Andrew Macfarlane

A Clinical Manual

a guide to the practical examination of the excretions, secretions, and the blood,

for the use of physicians and students

Andrew Macfarlane

A Clinical Manual
a guide to the practical examination of the excretions, secretions, and the blood, for the use of physicians and students

ISBN/EAN: 9783337390686

Printed in Europe, USA, Canada, Australia, Japan

Cover: Foto ©Andreas Hilbeck / pixelio.de

More available books at **www.hansebooks.com**

A CLINICAL MANUAL

A GUIDE TO THE PRACTICAL EXAMINATION
OF THE EXCRETIONS, SECRETIONS, AND
THE BLOOD, FOR THE USE OF
PHYSICIANS AND STUDENTS

BY

ANDREW MacFARLANE, A.B., M.D.

INSTRUCTOR IN NEUROLOGY AND DISEASES OF THE CHEST IN THE ALBANY MEDICAL
COLLEGE, PHYSICIAN TO ST. PETER'S HOSPITAL OUT-PATIENT DEPARTMENT
AND PHYSICIAN TO ALBANY'S HOSPITAL FOR INCURABLES

G. P. PUTNAM'S SONS

NEW YORK   LONDON
27 WEST TWENTY-THIRD STREET   24 BEDFORD STREET, STRAND

The Knickerbocker Press

1894

Electrotyped, Printed and Bound by
The Knickerbocker Press, New York
G. P. Putnam's Sons

PREFACE.

The last decade has witnessed the most marvellous advances in physiological chemistry, which, together with clinical microscopy, has done much to solve many of the problems coming daily to the attention of the physician. To-day the physician, to be successful, must be able to use the results of such work in his daily practice. This book has been written for the purpose of giving in a concise manner the methods employed in such investigation, not so full as to weary the busy physician, but sufficiently complete for all practical, clinical purposes. The object is not to make a chemist or a bacteriologist out of the clinician, but to add to his practical knowledge something which would assist him in diagnosticating diseased conditions. All the procedures, with a very few exceptions, are such as could be easily carried out by any physician in his own office with a suitable microscope and a small amount of apparatus.

The writer has not hesitated to cull from many sources, and desires to acknowledge his indebtedness to the works of Jaksch, Vierordt, Ewald, Leube, Eichhorst, Fraenkel, Bernheim, Limbeck, Rieder, Lenhartz, Halliburton, Osler, Councilman and Lafleur, Delafield and Prudden, and others, and especially to Tappeiner's *Anleitung zu Chemisch Diagnostischen Untersuchungen am Krankenbette*, after which this book has to some extent

iii

been modelled, and from which certain procedures have been directly translated.

The writer also wishes to express his thanks to Prof. T. Mitchell Prudden for his kindness in allowing him the use of the laboratory of the College of Physicians and Surgeons, New York City, and for his valuable suggestions and wise counsel ; to Dr. Wm. Halleck Park, who has kindly written the section on diphtheria, and whose work on that disease promises to yield noteworthy results ; to Gustavus Michaelis, Ph.D., who generously gave considerable time to correcting the manuscript ; and to several other friends who have aided him greatly with their advice.

ANDREW MACFARLANE.

ALBANY, N. Y.
April, 1894.

CONTENTS.

v

Part II.—THE STOMACH CONTENTS.

Part V.—PATHOLOGICAL FLUIDS.

Part VI.—PATHOGENIC MICRO-ORGANISMS.

LIST OF ILLUSTRATIONS.

A CLINICAL MANUAL.

Part I.—THE URINE.

I.—General Properties of the Urine.

1. CHANGES AFTER EXCRETION.—Normal urine when voided is transparent. It becomes slightly cloudy after standing, due to the presence of mucus and epithelium. After a time (over twenty-four hours) a sediment composed of uric acid, urates, and calcium oxalate is formed, if alkaline fermentation has not taken place within that time.

Alkaline fermentation usually occurs in twenty-four hours, though it may set in earlier or later than this. It appears most rapidly in faintly acid urine, in urine of low specific gravity, in urine containing albumin, blood, or mucus, and in urine collected in dirty vessels. The urine becomes cloudy and alkaline through the development and action of fungi,[1] which convert the urea into ammonium carbonate :

$$CH_4N_2O + 2\,H_2O = (N\,H_4)_2CO_3$$

urea   water   ammonium carbonate

As a result, a sediment composed of the earthy phosphates, ammonio-magnesium phosphates, and later of

---

[1] Principally of two kinds, micrococcus ureæ and bacterium ureæ.

ammonium urates is formed. The odor becomes pungent on account of the volatility of the ammonium carbonate.

2. QUANTITY.—The quantity of urine voided by a normal adult in twenty-four hours ranges from 1200–1500 c.c. (40–50 fluid ounces). It is, however, very variable in health, being complemental to the excretion by the lungs, the skin, and the bowels, and increased or diminished by an increase or decrease in drink and food.

It may sink in disease to nothing, anuria, or be increased to about 10,000 c.c. (338 fluid ounces), polyuria. In general it is in an inverse ratio to the specific gravity, to the intensity of the color, and to the degree of acidity. Highly colored, strongly acid urine has a high specific gravity, but the quantity is small. Pale, faintly acid urine has a low specific gravity, but the quantity is large. Pale urine of a high specific gravity and in increased quantity is indicative of diabetes mellitus.

3. COLOR.—The color of normal urine varies from a pale yellow to an amber yellow depending upon its degree of concentration ; the more concentrated, the darker the color. It may be altered either by a change in the normal urinary pigments or by the presence of abnormal coloring matters.

1. *The Urinary Pigments*, especially the urobilin, are increased :

relatively, by concentration of the urine ;
absolutely, by increased tissue metamorphosis, fever, and hemorrhage, when the hæmoglobin is converted into urobilin.
They are decreased by an increased proportion of water and in anæmia.
Pale urine, not increased in quantity, appears in convalescence after fevers.

2. *Abnormal Coloring Matter.*

(a) Those which normally exist in the organism but appear in the urine as a result of pathological changes.

1. The pigment of the blood—bright red to brownish black.
2. The pigment of the bile—yellowish green to brownish yellow.
3. Melanin (seldom)—brown to black.

The urine when excreted usually contains only melanogen and from this the pigment (melanin) is formed gradually by exposure to the air or rapidly by the action of an oxidizing agent.

(b) Color following the use of drugs or certain foods.

1. After the administration of carbolic acid, tar, leaves of uva ursa, and similar drugs, sulpho-acids and aromatic phenols are formed. These are colorless in themselves, but are easily oxidized and converted into greenish-black products as soon as the urine becomes alkaline (carboluria).

2. After the ingestion of rhubarb or senna, chrysophanic acid appears in the urine. The urine does not change in color while acid, but assumes a brown to blood-red color when alkaline.

3. After the administration of santonin the urine has a saffron to green color, resembling icteric urine. The addition of caustic soda to such urine produces a red color similar to that due to the use of rhubarb or senna (this differentiates it from biliary coloring mater).

4. REACTION.—Normal urine is acid, *colors blue litmus paper red*, due not to the free acids but to the acid salts, especially mono-sodium phosphate NaH_2PO_4 (acid sodium phosphate).

It may however be alkaline, *colors red litmus paper blue*, due to :

(a) The presence of the so-called fixed alkalies, *i.e.*, the non-volatile, alkaline phosphates and carbonates, viz. : di-sodium phosphate Na_2HPO_4, tri-sodium phosphate Na_3PO_4, and sometimes sodium carbonate Na_2CO_3. Such urine when excreted may be clear or cloudy, but after a short time it always becomes cloudy on account of the precipitation of the earthy phosphates $Ca_3(PO_4)_2$ and $Mg_3(PO_4)_2$ with which some crystals of ammonio-magnesium phosphate may be mixed.

The alkaline reaction of the litmus paper (change of color) does not disappear by drying the paper in the air.

(b) The presence of ammonium carbonate.

Such urine has undergone alkaline fermentation in the bladder and is in the same condition as urine which has undergone fermentation outside of the body.

It is cloudy from the presence of bacteria and of precipitated earthy phosphates with which many crystals of ammonio-magnesium phosphate are mixed.

The alkaline reaction of the litmus paper disappears upon drying the paper in the air (due to the volatilization of the ammonium carbonate).

Urine at the beginning of alkaline fermentation may give both reactions, *colors blue litmus paper red and red litmus paper blue,* caused principally by the presence, at the same time, of mono-sodium phosphate NaH_2PO_4 and di-sodium phosphate Na_2HPO_4, the former giving an acid, the latter an alkaline reaction.

CAUSES FOR THE FLUCTUATION IN THE REACTION OF THE URINE IN NORMAL AND PATHOLOGICAL CASES.

(c) The acidity of the urine is increased ;

1. When the urine is concentrated, *i.e.,* increased excretion of water by other channels than the kidneys, diminished consumption of fluids.

2. Increased metamorphosis of albumin (meat diet, self-consumption in fever).

(d) The acidity of the urine is lessened or entirely disappears :

1. Increased consumption of fluids.

2. Decreased metamorphosis of tissue (anæmia, debility).

3. Consumption of carbonates and alkalies of organic acids (citrates, malates, tartrates) which are converted into carbonates and pass into the urine (vegetable diet, sour wines, medicines, mineral waters).

4. Removal of acids from the blood by the secretion of the gastric juice, transitory at every meal, but permanent by continuous vomiting.

5. Rapid resorption of alkaline transudates and exudates.

6. Alkaline secretions in the urinary tract (cystitis, gonorrhœa, abscess, etc.).

7. Alkaline fermentation.

5. SPECIFIC GRAVITY.—The specific gravity of normal urine ranges from 1015–1025, the specific gravity of water being 1000. The pathological variations fluctuate from 1002–1040.

The specific gravity of a given portion of urine is a relative measure of the concentration of the urine. The amount of the solid constituents of the urine can be approximately estimated from the specific gravity of a mixture of the urine for the day, twenty-four hours, if the quantity of urine passed is known. Multiply the last two figures of the specific gravity by 2 (Trapp's coefficient) or 2.33 (Haser's coefficient). The product is the weight of the solid constituents in 34 fluid ounces (1000 c.c.) of the urine in grams (1 gram = 15.4 grains).

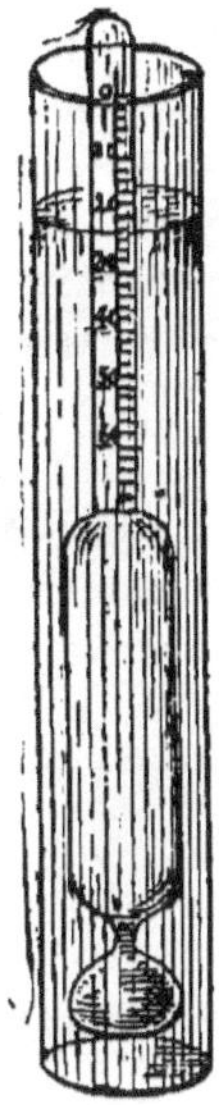

METHOD OF DETERMINATION. This is determined by the urinometer (Fig. 1) in the following manner: Fill the glass cylinder, usually sold with the urinometer, three

FIG. I.—URINOMETER.

quarters full of urine, which, if necessary, should first be filtered. The cylinder should be held inclined while it is being filled with urine to prevent the formation of foam. The urinometer, clean and dry, is slowly introduced so that the instrument swims entirely free in the urine. To determine accurately the specific gravity, bring the eye on a level with the lower border of the surface of the urine, and read off where it cuts the scale of the urinometer. This is accomplished as soon as the back border of the surface of the urine is no longer seen.

A dirty or wet instrument or solid particles suspended in the urine cause the specific gravity to appear too high.

A sensitive urinometer should permit correct reading to a half degree and have a scale extending from 1000, the weight of distilled water, to 1060. The urinometer gives exact results only at the temperature for which it has been constructed (usually 60° F.). The urine should have this temperature when an accurate determination is desired. For general practice, however, it is sufficient if the urine has nearly this temperature, *i. e.*, the temperature of the room. Warm urine has a lower, cold urine a higher specific gravity, a difference in temperature of 7° F. corresponding to one degree of the urinometer.

If the quantity of urine is not sufficient, it may be diluted with one, two, or more volumes of water. The specific gravity of the urine can then be easily determined by multiplying the last two figures of the specific gravity of the mixture by the total number of volumes in the mixture. Thus if three times as much water as urine have been added, and the specific gravity of the mixture is 1005, that of the urine is (05 x 4 = 20) 1020.

6. QUANTITATIVE COMPOSITION OF THE URINE.—The quantities of the urinary constituents excreted in twenty-four hours by an average man weighing 145 lbs. (Parkes).

	Grams.	Grains.
Water.....................	1500.	23,150.
Total Solids..............	72.	1,111.
Urea................	33.18	512.
Uric Acid...........	.55	8.5
Hippuric Acid........	.40	6.17
Creatinin............	.91	14.
Pigment and other organic substances	10.	154.
Sulphuric Acid........	2.01	31.
Phosphoric Acid......	3.16	48.76
Chlorine..............	7.00–8.00	108.–123.45
Ammonia	.77	11.88
Potassium............	2.50	38.58
Sodium..............	11.09	171.12
Calcium..............	0.26	4.01
Magnesium...........	0.21	3.24

7. THE SELECTION OF A SPECIMEN OF URINE.—As the properties of the urine vary during the twenty-four hours, exact analysis requires that the specimen for examination should be a part of the whole quantity passed during that time ; when this is not convenient the urine passed before breakfast is most suitable. If, however, traces of albumin are suspected, urine passed during the day, and especially after vigorous physical exertion, contains more albumin than urine passed after the body has been resting.

II.—Organic Substances.

I.—PROTEIDS.

8. ALBUMIN.—Albumin is a proteid substance, the chief constituent of the body, and occurs as serum-albumin, serum-globulin, muscle-albumin, fibrinogen, myosin, and the compounds, acid and alkaline albuminates. The albumin found in albuminuria consists usually of serum-albumin and serum-globulin, of which the serum-albumin is generally in much greater quantity.

Traces of albumin are at times found in the urine of healthy individuals, especially after vigorous muscular exertion, emotional excitement, and digestive disorders, while careful microscopic examinations show nothing, and the clinical symptoms of an acute or chronic disease of the kidneys are absent (*physiological albuminuria*). *A continuous excretion, however, of even the smallest quantity is always pathological.* Albuminuria may be the result of an admixture of albuminous fluids as blood, pus, chyle, though the urine itself is free from albumin. In such cases the urine usually contains only a small quantity of albumin, and invariably a sediment of elements characteristic of the fluid, as blood cells, pus cells, etc. (*accidental albuminuria*). It may also be due to the pressure of tumors or the pregnant uterus on the renal vein, and may occur in febrile conditions, nervous disorders (delirium tremens, epilepsy, concussion of the brain), in many constitutional diseases, and in diseases of the blood (*transitory albuminuria*). In contradistinction to these forms of albuminuria is the *renal albuminuria* due to parenchymatous changes in the kidney or to circulatory derangements, and characterized by the formation of an organized sediment in greater or less amounts (casts, renal epithelia, blood cells, etc.). It is impossible to distinguish the various forms of albuminuria by chemical analysis, as the albumin in all cases has the same chemical character. This problem must be solved by the microscopical examination of the sediment. *A diagnosis of renal disease should therefore never be made from albuminuria alone.*

The quantity of albumin in albuminous urine ranges from 0.1–1.0 per cent. or 1–15 grams (15–231 grains) in twenty-four hours. Larger quantities of albumin up to 30 grms (462 grains) are seldom found. But the smallest quantity is of diagnostic importance.

Urine containing albumin is usually frothy and often cloudy from the presence of bacteria or sediment. If the urine cannot be clarified by filtration, it should be shaken with calcined magnesia or a few drops of caustic soda should be added. A precipitate of magnesium or earthy phosphates results, and this takes up the cloudiness. This is usually unnecessary in ordinary examinations, as the tests employed for the detection of albumin will cause almost all the cloudiness due to unorganized sediment to disappear.

Cloudiness the result of organized sediment alone remains. It should always be determined if the urine to be examined is free from admixture with elements which may contain albumin (menstrual blood, fæces, sputa, semen, etc.).

9. THE FOLLOWING TESTS ARE THE MOST USEFUL IN DETERMINING THE PRESENCE OF ALBUMIN.

1. *Heat Test.*—Boil the top of a column of urine in a test-tube and add, if a precipitate forms or not, concentrated nitric acid (5–10 drops) until the urine has a strongly acid reaction. If the precipitate does not dissolve, or forms after the addition of nitric acid, it is due to albumin.

If albumin is present in small quantity, a turbidity appears ; if about .1 per cent. is present, a flaky precipitate forms, and if there is a very high percentage of albumin (3 per cent.) all the urine is converted into a solid mass. Too small a quantity of nitric acid may not precipitate albumin, especially if the urine is alkaline. Too great a quantity may redissolve the precipitate of albumin, particularly if the urine is again heated after the addition of the nitric acid, or if the nitric acid is added before the urine is boiled.

The effervescence after the addition of the acid is caused by the elimination of carbonic acid gas from the carbonates and often occurs in alkaline urine.

REASONS FOR THE ADDITION OF NITRIC ACID.

(a) Albumin, though present in urine, may not be coagulated by heat. This is a common occurrence in alkaline urine even when containing a moderate quantity of albumin. The albumin in such cases is converted into an alkaline albuminate which is not coagulated by heat but by nitric acid.

(b) Urine when heated may show a precipitate, although no albumin is present—earthy phosphates soluble in nitric acid.

Urine, faintly acid or slightly alkaline, holds in solution calcium and magnesium phosphates as di-phosphates. These are split up by heat into soluble mono-phosphates and insoluble tri-phosphates, which form a flaky precipitate resembling albumin.

$$4\,CaHPO_4 \quad = \quad Ca\,(H_2PO_4)_2 \quad + \quad Ca_3\,(PO_4)_2$$
Di-calcium phosphate   Mono-calcium phos.   Tri-calcium phos.

$$4\,MgHPO_4 \quad = \quad Mg\,(H_2PO_4)_2 \quad + \quad Mg_3\,(PO_4)_2$$
Di-magnesium phosphate Mono-magnesium phos. Tri-mag. phos.

As the triple phosphates are very soluble in acids, they are dissolved by nitric acid and cannot be confounded with albumin.

A similar precipitation follows when the urine holds hydrocalcium and hydromagnesium carbonate $Ca\,(CO_3H)_2$, $Mg\,(CO_3H)_2$, in solution as occurs with vegetarians. They are converted by heat into insoluble neutral carbonates $CaCO_3$, $MgCO_3$, and carbon dioxide CO_2. These precipitates are also very soluble in acids.

POSSIBLE SOURCE OF ERROR.—The formation of a precipitate, not albumin, is limited to the precipitation of resinous acids which appear in the urine after the administration of large quantities of the balsams, as urates and uric acid are very soluble upon the application of heat. If resinous acids are suspected, add two volumes of alcohol, which will dissolve resinous acids but not albumin. The alcohol should be added only when the urine is cold and does not contain more nitric acid than recommended, as otherwise the alcohol will be oxidized with a stormy effervescence.

2. *Nitric Acid Test (Heller's Ring Test).*—Pour carefully with a pipette into a test-tube containing concentrated nitric acid an equal quantity of urine, holding the test-tube as obliquely as possible, so that the fluids do not mix. If at the junction of the fluids a sharply limited white cloudiness in the shape of a ring appears immediately or after a few minutes, albumin is present.

Possible Sources of Error.—(a) Precipitation of nitrate of urea (large crystals). This occurs only in very concentrated urine and appears after some time. Previous dilution of the urine prevents it.

(b) Precipitation of acid urates (cloudiness in the shape of a ring somewhat above the junction of the fluids). This also happens only in concentrated urine. The uric acid is freed from its salts by the nitric acid and is in part precipitated as it is almost insoluble in cold water. This can be avoided by diluting the urine with 1-2 volumes of water. This ring is dissipated on the application of heat.

(c) Precipitation of resinous acids (ring-shaped cloudiness). They appear in urine as salts after large doses of balsam of copaiva, styrax, and turpentine, and are precipitated by nitric acid. Differentiate this from albumin by Test 1 or 4.

(d) Precipitation of albumose (an uncommon occurrence). *Vide* albumose.

(e) Colored Rings. The pigment of the urine is oxidized by the nitric acid. Every specimen of urine therefore, and especially the highly colored, will show at the junction of the urine and nitric acid a brownish-red ring; if indican is present, a violet ring; if bile pigment, Gmelin's reaction. All these rings can be easily distinguished from albumin by the absence of cloudiness.

3. *Acetic Acid and Ferrocyanide of Potassium Test.*— The urine is rendered strongly acid with acetic acid (5 drops) and 1-3 drops of a ten-per-cent. solution of ferrocyanide of potassium are added. If albumin is present, a turbidity or flaky precipitate appears.

This test is the most delicate of all, especially when made in the same manner as the preceding test, *i. e.*, a mixture consisting of a drachm or two of diluted acetic acid and a few drops of ferrocyanide of potassium is carefully poured with a pipette upon the urine in a test-tube. If the slightest trace of albumin is present, a white ring forms at the junction of the liquids.

Mistakes are possible by the precipitation of mucin, resinous acid, and uric acid on the addition of the acid. The possibility of the reaction of the first two can be eliminated as in the following test and that of uric acid by diluting the urine with one or two volumes of water before testing. When the quantity of albumin is very small, the precipitate appears after a few minutes. If the urine is highly concentrated, the precipitate often does not appear until the urine has been diluted with an equal volume of water as it is somewhat soluble in a strongly acid solution.

4. *Acetic Acid, Sodium Chloride, and Heat Test.*— Acidulate strongly the urine with acetic acid (5 drops), add at least $\frac{1}{8}$ volume of a saturated solution of sodium chloride and boil the mixture.

If a precipitate forms first during the boiling, albumin is present.

If a precipitate appears on the addition of acetic acid it may be due to:

(a) Uric acid freed from its salts by acetic acid and precipitated in concentrated urine. The precipitate is redissolved by heat owing to its great solubility and is formed again so slowly, as acetic acid is a weak acid, that it is not usually observed.

(b) Resinous acids precipitated from their salts by the acid. The precipitate when heated does not disappear, in fact it may be more pronounced as the chemical action of acetic acid is intensified by heating. It can, however, be easily distinguished from albumin by the addition of alcohol after the urine becomes cold.

(c) Mucin. The precipitate does not form when sodium chloride is added first and then the acetic acid.

This test has these advantages: the color of the urine is not changed, the albumin is precipitated in heavier flakes, and the filtrate can be used for other tests, *e. g.*, sugar. Larger quantities of sodium chloride than ⅛ volume often precipitate the albumin before the urine is heated, as albumin in a concentrated solution of sodium chloride is rapidly converted into an acid albumin which is precipitated by acetic acid and sodium chloride.

10. QUANTITATIVE ESTIMATION OF ALBUMIN.— Exact quantitative estimation is possible by weighing the coagulated albumin separated by filtration, or by measuring the deflection to the left of the polarization line in urine containing albumin. The latter method gives exact results only for urine containing more than .5 per cent. of albumin and is rendered difficult by turbidity and high color of the urine, and the former requires more time than the general practitioner can give.

An approximate estimation, which can be easily made, is sufficiently accurate for practical purposes.

1. *Heat and Nitric Acid.*—The simplest method is to boil a quantity of urine in a test-tube, add a few drops of nitric acid, and set aside for 12 hours. If a small quantity of albumin is present, a turbidity results; if about one tenth per cent., a flaky precipitate forms, which, after settling, fills the curved bottom of the test-tube; if about one per cent., the precipitate in bulk makes up about one half of the volume of urine, and if the percentage of albumin is very high (3 per cent.), the urine is converted into a solid mass.

2. *Brandberg's Method.*—This method is based upon the fact that Test 2 (Heller's ring test) shows the reaction for albumin the more quickly, the richer the urine is in albumin. If there is only one part of albumin in 30,000 of urine, the turbidity appears in 2½ to 3 minutes.

If urine contains an unknown quantity of albumin, it can be easily determined, sufficiently exactly for clinical purposes, by diluting the urine with a known quantity of water until the reaction ensues in 2½ to 3 minutes. This diluted urine contains .0033 per cent. of albumin, and from this the per cent. of albumin in the undiluted urine is quickly calculated.

PROCEDURE.—Concentrated nitric acid is carefully poured with a pipette, so that the acid does not touch the sides of the tubes, into four test-tubes. Equal volumes of urine of different degrees of dilution are gently placed with a pipette upon the nitric acid, a different dilution in each test-tube, and the time is noted before a visible bluish-white ring appears in each test-tube. If the reaction occurs in 2½ to 3 minutes in one of them, this dilution of the urine contains .0033 per cent. of albumin. The quantity of albumin is then quickly ascertained from the following table.

Dilution of the urine.								Per cent. of albumin in the undiluted urine when the ring appears after 2½ to 3 minutes.
*10 times = 1 part urine, 9 parts water							.	0.033

(10 per cent. solution of urine used for the other dilutions.)

20 times = 1	part of above	dilution	+	1 part water	= 0.067
*30 " = 1	"	"	"	+	2 "	"	= 0.100
50 " = 1	"	"	"	+	4 "	"	= 0.167
80 " = 1	"	"	"	+	7 "	"	= 0.267
100 " = 1	"	"	"	+	9 "	"	= 0.333
*150 " = 1	"	"	"	+	14 "	"	= 0.500
200 " = 1	"	"	"	+	19 "	"	= 0.667
*300 " = 1	"	"	"	+	29 "	"	= 1.000
400 " = 1	"	"	"	+	39 "	"	= 1.333
500 " = 1	"	"	"	+	49 "	"	= 1.667

It is well not to make all the dilutions, but first to test those dilutions marked with an asterisk, and thus determine if the quantity of albumin is more or less than $\frac{1}{10}$ or $\frac{1}{2}$ or 1 per cent. Then to estimate exactly, it is only necessary to examine the dilutions between the limits determined.

The first dilution can be easily made by adding 5 parts of urine measured in a pipette to 45 of water ; the others are readily prepared from this.

3. *Esbach's Method.*—The measurement of the quantity of precipitated albumin in an especially constructed test-tube (albuminimeter).

REAGENT.—A solution of picric acid 10 grams (154 grains), and pure citric acid 20 grams (308 grains), in a litre (33.8 ounces) of water. This precipitates all the albumin except in some very rare cases which have not yet been explained. It also precipitates kreatinin, uric acid, and alkaloids, but this seldom makes any practical difference.

PROCEDURE.—Fill the tube (Figure 2) up to the mark U with urine, which should be fresh and acid, and add the reagent to the mark R. Close the tube with the thumb and mix the contents carefully, inverting it several times, so that no foam is formed. Cork the tube and place it aside upright for 24 hours. The albumin gradually sinks to the bottom and in 24 hours the quantity can be determined by the scale of the albuminimeter marked from 1–7. These figures indicate the quantity of albumin in grams in a litre of urine or the decimal percentage of albumin. When the urine is very rich in albumin it should be diluted with one or two volumes of water and the result multiplied by two or three. The Esbach method gives exact results for a quantity of albumin as small as 0.1 per cent. and on account of its simplicity answers sufficiently well for all ordinary requirements.

11. SEPARATION OF THE ALBUMIN.—It is necessary for many of the other examinations to separate the albumin present from the urine. This is easily accomplished even when the quantity is unimportant, by heating the urine rendered moderately acid and filtering.

FIG. 2.— ESBACH'S ALBUMIN-IMETER.

The urine when acid (neutral or alkaline urine is first weakly acidulated with diluted acetic acid) should be heated to the boiling point and then removed from the flame. If a heavy precipitate of albumin does not immediately form, but simply a cloudiness appears, as is usually the case, a few drops of diluted acetic acid should be carefully added until a flaky precipitate results.   The fluid should be again heated for a moment and at once filtered.   Complete coagulation is accomplished when the albumin is precipitated in large flakes and the fluid above is clear and runs quickly through the filter.   When turbid, too little or too much acetic acid has been added.   The first is easily corrected, and the second can be by neutralizing the excess of acid by the careful addition of a diluted solution of soda.   It is easier, however, to re-examine a fresh specimen of urine.

If urine or other liquids contain a large quantity of albumin, the following modification is valuable : Boil 20–30 c. c. (one ounce) of water in a small porcelain dish, add slowly, keeping the mixture at boiling point, one half to one volume of urine and stir continuously. The reaction is ascertained, and if necessary acetic acid is added until it is faintly acid.   A large flaky precipitate forms and is immediately filtered.

The precipitation of albumin by acetic acid is often used as a test for albumin, but it is not suitable unless very carefully employed. Too much acetic acid may dissolve a large part of the albumin, and even all if merely traces of albumin are present.

12. FIBRIN.—Fibrin is found in cases of hæmaturia and chyluria and occasionally as a result of irritation of the kidneys after the use of cantharides and of an inflammatory exudation in the urinary tract.   It is either coagulated in the urine when passed or precipitated by standing, and forms a flaky sediment or a thick coagulum.

Fibrin shows the characteristics of coagulated albumin, insolubility in water and saline solutions as well as in diluted acids and alkalies. It is converted in the cold by alkalies into a thick coagulum which dissolves after prolonged heating.   Solutions of fibrin react to the tests for albumin.

13. NUCLEO-ALBUMIN (MUCIN).—This body, formerly called mucin, now nucleo-albumin, is probably in small

quantities a normal product of the mucous membrane of the urinary tract, but when found in increased quantity it indicates a catarrhal condition. It is recognized on account of its precipitation by acetic acid and its weak solubility in an excess of the acid, especially if few salts are present.

Dilute the urine with 1-2 volumes of water and add acetic acid. If nucleo-albumin is present, a marked cloudiness results. This disappears on the addition of caustic soda and reappears when more acetic acid is added.

14. ALBUMOSE.—Albumose, an intermediate product between albumin and peptone, has repeatedly been detected in the urine in different diseases as osteomalacia, intestinal ulcer, and especially, in often large quantity, in multiple myeloma. It has also been found in urine containing the seminal fluid as albumose is a constituent of that secretion.

Urine containing albumose shows the following reactions :

(1) Urine rendered weakly acid, if necessary, with acetic acid becomes cloudy when heated to 60° C. (140° F.), clear when boiling, and again cloudy when cold.

(2) A few drops of nitric acid are added to urine which has been boiled (as in Test 1 for albumin). A precipitate appears when the solution is cold. It is dissolved by heat and reappears when cold.

(3) A small quantity of acetic acid and a few drops of a solution of ferrocyanide of potassium produce a cloudiness distinguished from albumin by its solubility in heated solution and its reappearance when the solution is cold.

(4) Sodium chloride in crystals added to saturation produces a precipitate which dissolves on the addition of acetic acid and the application of heat. If albumin is present, the precipitate remains or then forms. It should be filtered while hot and allowed to cool. If the precipitate re-forms albumose is present.

2

15. PEPTONE.—Small quantities of peptone have been found, though not invariably, in the urine of cases characterized by a rapid retrograde metamorphosis of normal and pathological tissues, *e. g.*, in the involution of the puerperal uterus, in acute atrophy of the liver, and phosphorus poisoning, after hemorrhages, in carcinoma, phthisis, croupous pneumonia, extensive exudates, and in nearly all suppurative conditions.

It is very soluble in water, does not coagulate when boiled, and shows no reaction with the majority of the common reagents employed for the detection of albumin—nitric acid, acetic acid + sodium chloride, acetic acid + ferrocyanide of potassium. It is precipitated by metaphosphoric acid, phospho-tungstic acid, potassio-mercuric iodide + acetic acid. These reactions cannot, however, be employed for the special determination of peptone in urine, as they are neither characteristic nor sufficiently sensitive. It must first be isolated and then tested. The method of Hofmeister is the one commonly employed.

Hofmeister's Test.—A large quantity of urine (20 ounces), which has been found free from albumin, is treated with neutral acetate of lead and then filtered. The filtrate is acidulated with hydrochloric acid and phospho-tungstic acid [1] is added until a precipitate ceases to form, and it is then immediately filtered. The precipitate, which contains peptone combined with phospho-tungstic acid and also other substances, is washed, in order to remove the salts present on the filter, with a solution of 5 parts of concentrated sulphuric acid in 100 parts of water, until the fluid passing through is colorless. The precipitate is removed from the filter with as little water as possible

---

[1] Phospho-tungstic acid is made by dissolving tungstate of soda in boiling water and adding phosphoric acid until the solution is acid. When cold it is rendered strongly acid with hydrochloric acid, and after standing for twenty-four hours is filtered.

into a porcelain dish and barium carbonate is added until the mixture becomes alkaline. It is then placed on a water-bath at the
boiling point and heated for 10–15 minutes and the biuret test
applied. This test consists of the addition of caustic potash and a
drop or two of a diluted (10 %) solution of sulphate of copper. A
bluish-red to violet color appears if peptone is present.

If the urine contains albumin, it should be removed by combining
it with iron oxide. The urine is treated with a solution of acetate
of soda and then with one of chloride of iron and exactly neutralized
with caustic potash, then boiled, filtered, and when cold examined for
albumin by Tests 1 and 3 (heat and acetic acid + ferrocyanide of
potassium tests). If both are negative and no blue color (due to iron)
results with Test 3, it should be examined for peptone, as described
above. If the tests show that a trace of albumin is present, the
removal of the albumin must be repeated until no albumin or iron can
be detected.

16. BLOOD IN THE URINE.—The color of the urine may
be yellowish-red, red, brown, or brownish-black, depending upon the quantity and form of hæmoglobin.
The hæmoglobin may have the form of oxy-hæmoglobin
(red urine); met-hæmoglobin (brown urine), and may
appear

(a) dissolved in the urine (hæmoglobinuria),

(b) enclosed in red blood corpuscles (hæmaturia).

This must be determined by the microscopical examination.

The pigment of the blood is oxy-hæmoglobin in all
excessive hemorrhages from the bladder; met-hæmoglobin in all forms of hæmoglobinuria, in many hemorrhages from the kidneys, and in slight hemorrhages from
the bladder. The presence of hæmoglobin in any quantity is recognized by the red color of the urine. The
met-hæmoglobin is after a time converted into oxy-
hæmoglobin or reduced hæmoglobin. The presence of

hæmoglobin may be determined by the spectroscopic examination or by various tests.

Spectroscopic Examination.

OXY-HÆMOGLOBIN.—Its aqueous solutions are characterized by a bright-red color and two absorption lines in the spectrum. These are easily recognized in a layer of diluted urine (even to 0.01 per cent.) $\frac{1}{2}$–1 inch thick with a good pocket spectroscope and bright daylight (Fig. 3, A and B).

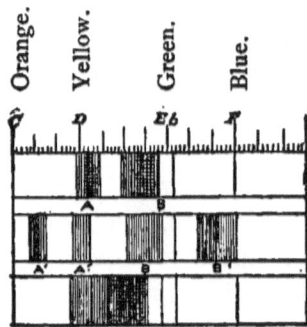

Spectrum of
Oxy-hæmoglobin.

Met-hæmoglobin.

Reduced hæmoglobin.

FIG. 3.

MET-HÆMOGLOBIN.—This has the same quantity of oxygen as oxy-hæmoglobin, but in stronger union. It is formed from oxy-hæmoglobin by the addition of acids and acid salts (hence its presence in urine). It is characterized in acid and neutral solutions by its brown color and by two more lines in the spectrum ; all four lines (Fig. 3, AA' BB') are visible only when a large percentage of met-hæmoglobin is present. If the solution is greatly diluted the line A' alone appears.

REDUCED HÆMOGLOBIN.—This is formed from the two just described by de-oxidation. It is characterized in moderately weak solutions by a greenish, brownish, red color, and by a broad, ill-defined absorption line (Fig. 3). On shaking with air it is transformed into oxy-hæmoglobin.

Hæmoglobin, when boiled or treated with acids or alkalies, is split up into hæmatin and albumin. Hæmatin is amorphous, of a brownish-black color, insoluble in water and acids, very soluble in alkalies, somewhat soluble in warm glacial acetic acid, out of which it separates in characteristic rhomboidal crystals (hæmin crystals, Fig. 4) when a crystal of sodium chloride is added.

1. *Heat Test.*—Boil the urine ; a brown coagulum forms ; not sensitive. If the urine is alkaline there is often merely a brown coloration and the coagulum forms only after the addition of acetic acid.

2. *Heller's Test.*—The urine is made alkaline with caustic soda and then boiled. A flaky blood-red precipitate of the earthy phosphates results.

If the quantity of hæmoglobin is small the precipitate becomes visible only when it sinks to the bottom of the tube.

This reaction is based upon the formation of hæmatin which is taken up by the earthy phosphates precipitated by the alkali. In urine free from the pigment of the blood, the precipitate of the phosphates is white. Dark-brown flakes form when too little or too much caustic soda has been added or when the solution is over-heated. These are not so readily recognized as the blood-red, but are equally characteristic.

Frequently in alkaline urine no precipitate forms, especially if all the calcium phosphate has settled as sediment. In such cases the test should be repeated with the addition of a calcic salt.

After the use of chrysarobin, rhubarb, and senna, a yellow pigment (chrysophanic acid) appears in the urine. This becomes red in alkaline urine, and when heated is precipitated in red flakes with the phosphates. The differentiation is easy. The precipitate of the phosphates is soluble in acetic acid, while the hæmatin remains in dark-brown flakes. Such urine can also be examined by Tests 1, 3, and 4. If a large quantity of chrysophanic acid is present, it may be recognized by the red color of the urine, especially the foam, upon the addition of caustic soda.

The urine gives the same reaction after the administration of santonin. Differentiate by No. 39.

3. *Almen's Test.*—An emulsion of freshly prepared tincture of guaiac and oxidized (*i. e.*, old and exposed to the air) oil of turpentine, equal parts, is carefully poured upon the urine. At the junction of the fluids a white ring, due to the precipitation of resin, forms. If hæmoglobin is present, the ring is immediately colored a beautiful blue.

This test is even more sensitive than the spectral test for hæmoglobin. Its action depends on the transference of the ozone of the oil of turpentine to the guaiac resin by the hæmoglobin, thus oxidizing (coloring blue) the guaiac.

It should be kept in mind that the guaiac resin is colored blue by pus even without the addition of turpentine. When the urine is alkaline the test is less sensitive. It is therefore well to acidulate with acetic acid before testing. A tincture of one part of guaiac resin and eighteen parts of alcohol makes a very sensitive reagent. This should be made up as required, or at least kept in a dark glass bottle. The oil of turpentine should be exposed in a half-filled bottle to the light. The reagents should occasionally be tested with urine to which blood has been added.

4. *Test for Hæmin Crystals.*—The precipitate obtained by test 1 or 2 is collected on a small filter, washed thoroughly, and dried by gentle heat. Place a small quantity upon a slide, add to it a crystal of sodium chloride, and lay upon it a cover glass. Allow a few drops of glacial acetic acid to flow beneath the cover

glass, and heat the preparation over a small flame for a minute to a point below boiling. Replace the glacial acetic acid, as it evaporates, with fresh acid, drop by drop.   If hæmatin is present, the fluid gradually becomes brownish-red.   When this oc- curs, remove the preparation some distance from the flame until it cools and the glacial acetic acid evaporates. Look

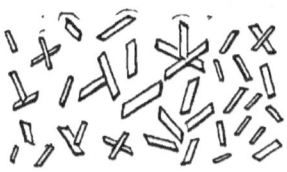

FIG. 4.—HÆMIN CRYSTALS.

for the crystals of hæmin (Fig. 4) when the objective of the microscope has been focused on the brown spots. Beautiful preparations of hæmin crystals may be obtained by gently evaporating a drop of blood on a slide and treating it in the manner just described.

II.—COLORING MATTERS.

17. BILE-PIGMENTS.—The presence of biliary acids in the urine can be detected only by methods so tedious as to be useless for clinical purposes. When Petten- kofer's test with cane sugar and sulphuric acid is employed, the presence of bodies which yield a similar violet-red color, renders the result so uncertain that 0.5 per cent. of biliary acid must be present, which rarely occurs in icterus, to secure an undoubted reaction.

The recognition, however, of the presence of the bile- pigments is a comparatively simple matter, and therefore of much more clinical importance.   The bile-pigments are bilirubin (yellow or brown) and biliverdin (green). They are insoluble in water and acids, soluble in alkalies from which they are precipitated in reddish-brown or green flakes by salts of lime. They form with lime compounds insoluble in water (such is the combination in gall-stones).

BILIRUBIN is insoluble in alcohol, soluble with a yellow coloration in chloroform, and crystallizes out of it in brownish-red prisms and small plates.

BILIVERDIN is on the contrary insoluble in chloroform, but soluble in alcohol, out of which it crystallizes in imperfectly defined shapes.

Icteric urine is yellowish-green to dark-brown, and when shaken shows a yellow foam. The sediment present (oxalate of calcium, casts, epithelium) often has a beautiful yellow color.

1. *Gmelin's Test.*—Filter some urine and touch the inner side of the still wet filtering paper with a drop of yellow concentrated nitric acid. If bile-pigment is present, concentric color-rings appear on the spot touched, on the outside a green, then blue, violet, red, and yellow rings.

This test proposed by Rosenbach is a very sensitive modification of the original Gmelin's test, in which the urine is carefully poured on concentrated nitric acid, and the same play of colors appears in the form of rings one above another. The sensitiveness of the test increases with the quantity of urine filtered. Not less than 50–100 c.c. (2–3 ounces) should be filtered.

This reaction is the result of the oxidation of bilirubin into other pigments of which biliverdin (green color) results first. The reaction is possible only when the nitric acid has a yellow color, *i. e.*, holds some nitrous acid. This results from the long exposure of nitric acid to light, or more rapidly by heating it with a small piece of wood or sugar.

The filtering paper used must be free from impurities. If it contains coloring matter, this may show the reaction with nitric acid. It should be tested before being used with a drop of nitric acid.

All specimens of urine, though highly colored, and certainly icteric, do not react positively to Gmelin's test. If little bile pigment is present, the play of colors may be entirely hidden by other pigments, urobilin, and the like. In such cases either the urobilin should first be separated from the urine by acidulating and shaking with chloroform, in which it is dissolved, with a yellow coloration, or the following special tests may be employed.

2. *Huppert's Test.*—Add to urine lime-water or a solution of barium chloride + caustic soda. The resulting precipitate is separated by filtration and boiled with alcohol, to which a few drops of diluted sulphuric acid have been added : a beautiful green solution results if bile-pigment is present ; a deep rose color if urobilin is contained in the urine ; a bluish-gray precipitate at the outset and later not a green, but, if any, a yellow or reddish color results if indican is present.

3. *Stokois's Test.*—20–30 c.c. (one ounce) of urine are precipitated by 5–10 c. c. (1–2½ drachms) of a 20 per cent. solution of zinc acetate. The precipitate is collected on filtering paper, washed, and dissolved in ammonia water. The solution assumes immediately or after exposure to the air a brownish-green color with fluorescence, and presents in the spectrum the characteristic absorption bands of cholecyanin (bilicyanin), viz., a sharp line at c, a faint one at D, and a very faint one between D and E.

4. *Iodine Test.*—Pour carefully with a pipette upon urine in a test-tube, a drachm of a diluted (10 per cent.) alcoholic solution of the tincture of iodine. If bile-pigment is present, a grass-green ring forms at the plane of contact of the two fluids. If no bile-pigment is present, only a light-yellow or colorless ring appears.

18. Urobilin.—Urobilin is the result of a metamorphosis of the pigment of the blood, and also of a reduction of bilirubin, and therefore also called hydrobilirubin.

It is an amorphous, reddish-brown substance, soluble with difficulty in water, very soluble in alcohol, chloroform, and alkalies ; it forms insoluble salts with the earthy and heavy metals, and does not react to Gmelin's test for bile-pigment. Small quantities are present even in normal urine in the form of a chromogen, which is easily converted into urobilin, especially in the presence of acids. It is found in large quantity in cases characterized by disintegration of red corpuscles, as after fever and extravasation of blood (cerebral hemorrhage, hemorrhagic infarct, retro-uterine hematocele, extra-uterine pregnancy, scorbutus, etc.). It may also occur in hepatic disease, most commonly in hepatic cirrhosis and congestion. The urine in these cases is always of an intensely brownish-red color, and often has a yellow foam like icteric urine.

1. *Spectral Test.*—Urine rich in urobilin shows an absorption line between green and blue answering about to the position of the fourth met-hæmoglobin line (Fig. 3, b'). The line is more distinct in acid than in alkaline urine, in which it is deflected to the left.

2. *Fluorescence Test.*—Five drops of a 10 per cent. solution of chloride of zinc are added to the urine, then ammonia until the precipitate formed is dissolved by shaking. If urobilin is present in not too small a quantity, a green fluorescence becomes visible when it is held against a dark background after the precipitated phosphates have settled.

Urobilin is in this reaction precipitated as a zinc salt and then redissolved by the ammonia. All solutions of urobilin are fluorescent. Urine very rich in urobilin often exhibits this property before it is tested. The solutions of zinc salts possess this characteristic in a marked degree.

Very small quantities of urobilin cannot be recognized in urine. The urobilin must first be isolated by shaking the acidulated urine with chloroform, and then abstracted by treating it with a diluted solution of caustic soda.

19. INDICAN (*Indoxyl-sulphuric acid $C_8H_6NOSO_2OH$*). —A product of albuminoid retrograde metamorphosis in

the intestinal canal, and therefore, in small quantities, a normal element. It appears in large quantities in a meat diet, simple constipation, digestive disorders, carcinoma of the stomach, liver, or ileum, typhoid fever, tuberculosis of the intestine, peritonitis, and in internal suppuration.

Jaffe's Test.—Fill a test-tube one half with urine, add an almost equal quantity of concentrated hydrochloric acid, then 2–3 c.c. (½ drachm) of chloroform and one drop of a moderately saturated solution of chloride of lime. Mix by inverting the test-tube, closed with the thumb, a number of times. If indican is present, a blue coloration appears in the lower part of the fluid.

This reaction is due to the splitting of indican into indoxyl and sulphuric acid by the hydrochloric acid and the oxidation of the indoxyl into indigo blue by the lime. The indigo blue, insoluble in water, is precipitated as a finely divided blue sediment and is taken up by the chloroform. If more lime be added drop by drop, the blue color disappears when there is but little indican present, as the indican is further oxidized to yellow isatin. If the urine is very rich in indican, the blue color is at first intensified, and then, after the addition of more of the solution of lime, changes to a yellow. This characteristic allows an approximate quantitative estimation of indican to be easily made. The shaking with chloroform should not be vigorous, as an emulsion will be formed with the urine.

Urine containing albumin should have previously been freed from it. A 1–2 per cent. solution of permanganate of potassium may be employed instead of the lime, but it must be mixed longer with the chloroform and frequently added until the maximum of color results.

III.—GRAPE SUGAR (DEXTROSE).

20. GLYCOSURIA.—Grape sugar has often (18 in 100 cases) been found in small quantity in normal urine, and especially after the consumption of an unusual

quantity of sugar (*physiological glycosuria*) ; it may be the result of an excretion of milk sugar in the urine of nursing mothers (*lactosuria*), and may also occur as an occasional and temporary accompaniment of many diseases, as infectious diseases, diseases of the heart and lungs, cirrhosis of the liver, and nervous disorders (*transitory glycosuria*).

An increased secretion of sugar, which cannot be attributed to any of the above causes, which is a continuous condition (*persistent glycosuria*) with a mixed diet, diminishes or disappears under a meat diet, increases under a diet rich in carbo-hydrates, is the most certain and usually the earliest symptom of diabetes mellitus.

The quantity of sugar found in the urine in diabetes mellitus is usually not more than 4 per cent. ; in very severe cases 5–6 per cent. ; and very rarely a larger quantity up to 10 per cent. (500 grams daily).

Whenever urine has a specific gravity of 1020 or more, is very pale, clear, and without sediment, and increased in amount, it should be examined for sugar.

1. *Test of Moore and Heller.*—Add to the urine in a test-tube $\frac{1}{4}$–$\frac{1}{3}$ its volume of caustic soda and boil 2–3 minutes. If sugar is present, the urine becomes a dark-yellow to a dark-brown, the color varying with the quantity of sugar.

This reaction is due to the oxidation of the grape sugar, and is very sensitive in a solution of pure sugar. In urine, however, it is characteristic of sugar only when a large quantity of sugar is present —*i. e.*, when the pronounced brown color appears, as the dark-yellow color can be produced by heating urine, free from sugar, with caustic soda.

The flaky precipitate usually observed in this test consists of the earthy phosphates. These are precipitated in the cold by the caustic soda and form, when heated, large flakes. This is a normal condition.

2. *Trommer's Test.*—Add to the urine $\frac{1}{4}$ its volume of caustic soda, and with strong shaking a solution of cupric sulphate drop by drop until a small quantity of copper remains undissolved. If the urine dissolves much copper and at the same time assumes a beautiful blue color, the presence of sugar is probable.

Then heat to just below the boiling point (the upper part of the solution only should be heated) ; if the part heated shows yellowish-red lines or heavy flakes of pre-cipitated cupric suboxide separated sharply from the rest of the fluid which continues blue, and if this precipitate gradually forms through the entire solution, the presence of sugar is proved.

Trommer's test acts in this typical way only in pronounced dia-betic urine. In many cases the urine dissolves a large quantity of cupric oxide, the blue color is changed on heating to a yellow or brown ; a precipitation of cupric suboxide does not, however, result, or it occurs only after a long time (a brown precipitate of the earthy phosphates with some cupric oxide may lead to error). It is often possible in such cases to obtain, by exact saturation with cupric sulphate, a precipitate while the solution is being heated.

It is often very difficult to decide when the sulphate of copper, which is being added, ceases to be dissolved, as a marked cloudiness appears in many specimens of urine immediately after the addition of the caustic soda. In such cases it is advisable to carry out Trommer's test in the following manner :

Add to a quantity of urine, sufficient for 4 tests, caustic soda and cupric sulphate as described, until the solution seems saturated with sulphate of copper. Pour $\frac{1}{4}$ of this mixture into a test-tube and heat it. If no precipitate of suboxide forms while a yellow coloration appears, add to the remaining parts some additional cupric sulphate and test $\frac{1}{3}$ of this mixture ; continue adding cupric sulphate to the remainder and testing in the same manner until a precipitate of suboxide forms or until the solution has, after heating, a permanent green color, indicating a surplus of copper which cannot be reduced. In the first case the presence of sugar is proved, in the second Trommer's test leaves the question in doubt as this reduction (change of color) may be due to sugar or may be caused by other reducing substances. Positive differentiation is possible only by tests 3, 4, or 5.

An answer to the questions—why the precipitation of cupric suboxide does not always follow, why it must occur for proof of sugar, and why the color reaction alone is not sufficient?—is given by a knowledge of the chemical principles underlying these reactions and of their relation to normal urine. It will thus become evident how absolutely necessary it is to adhere strictly to the directions in making this test.

Reaction between caustic soda and cupric sulphate. 1. Add to water caustic soda and a solution of cupric sulphate, a heavy blue precipitate of cupric hydroxide forms $CuSO_4 + 2NaOH = Na_2SO_4 + Cu(OH)_2$. This is insoluble in caustic soda and when heated is converted into a brownish black cupric oxide CuO, more accurately $Cu(OH)_2 + 2CuO$.

Substances which dissolve cupric oxide. 2. If the water contains certain substances as glycerine, tartrates, ammonia, albumin, or grape sugar, the precipitate of cupric hydroxide is dissolved, by shaking, into a blue liquid. This property of dissolving cupric oxide is therefore not a characteristic of grape sugar alone.

3. The blue color in the above solution when boiled is affected differently ; if glycerine, tartaric acid, ammonia, or albumin is present no change ensues, but if sugar is present a yellow or red precipitate of cupric suboxide immediately forms and the solution assumes this color.

Different results when heated.

This phenomenon is due to the oxidation of the sugar. The sugar in heated alkaline solution attracts from the cupric oxide a part of its oxygen and converts it into red cupric suboxide Cu_2O or yellow cupric suboxide hydrate $Cu_2(OH)_2$.

This property of reducing cupric oxide is, however, not peculiar to grape sugar alone as many organic bodies share with it this characteristic. They are called by the generic term reducing substances.

Reducing substances.

Some of the reducing substances are found in the urine and their presence in normal urine is easily detected by Trommer's test. This leads to the recognition of an important property of normal urine.

4. If caustic soda is added to normal urine, a precipitate of earthy phosphates forms. This is scarcely visible at first, but gradually falls to the bottom in colorless flakes. If a solution of cupric sulphate is now added drop by drop, each drop will produce a heavy blue precipitate of cupric hydroxide which is redissolved by shaking. If cupric sulphate is added until a small quantity of the copper (3 to 5 drops) remains insoluble, and if the resulting bluish-green solution is boiled, the color is changed into yellow when examined by reflected light, and to a reddish-yellow by refracted light. The cupric oxide has been reduced but the copper is not precipitated as the fluid remains perfectly clear. The precipitate of the phosphates is clearly visible, and after it sinks to the bottom it is of a reddish-brown color, due to traces of cupric suboxide which accompany it.

Power of normal urine to dissolve and reduce cupric oxide.

This reaction shows :

(a) That the normal urine contains substances which dissolve cupric oxide (uric acid, kreatinin, salts of ammonia).

(b) That it contains substances which reduce cupric oxide (uric acid, pyrocatechin, etc.).

(c) That it contains substances which dissolve cupric sub-oxide (uric acid, kreatinin, salts of ammonia, etc.). The power of the normal urine to dissolve and reduce cupric oxide is not great and is overcome by 3 to 5 drops of cupric sulphate. Much more important is the power to dissolve cupric suboxide as the following experiment shows.

5. Add to normal urine about 0.5 per cent. of grape sugar and proceed as before. The same phenomena ensue but more markedly ; a fairly strong solution of CuO, a pronounced yellow coloration on heating, but no precipitation of cupric suboxide during or immediately

after heating.   The cause of this phenomenon is the great power of the normal urine to dissolve cupric suboxide (Cu_2O) on account of which not only the suboxide which the reducing bodies have formed, but also that due to the oxidation of the sugar, will be held in solution.   The precipitate will first appear when the quantity of sugar is very large and much cupric suboxide is formed of which all is not dissolved.

6.   The normal urine, to which 0.5 per cent. sugar has been added, acts in the same manner as the previously described pathological urine with incomplete action of Trommer's test (failure of the precipitation of cupric suboxide).   Such urine **The precipitation of cupric suboxide is alone proof of sugar.** may contain sugar but there is no proof of it, as the reduction may be due to other reducing substances, which, as has been shown, are present in greater or less quantity in urine.

When the precipitation of cupric suboxide is added to its reduction, the presence of sugar is proved, as it is known from experience that no other reducing body, which can produce a precipitate of cupric suboxide, is present in the urine.

7.   The conclusion that sugar is present from the precipitation of cupric suboxide is permitted only when the temperature during the test remains below the boiling **Necessity of keeping the temperature below the boiling point.** point.   Therefore urine should be heated to just below the boiling point.   Boiling, especially when prolonged, may produce a precipitate of cupric suboxide in many specimens of normal urine, usually, however, not during the boiling but only after it has become cold.

8.   As the urine contains bodies capable of dissolving cupric suboxide, it is necessary, especially when the quantity of sugar is small and the urine concentrated, to obtain the formation of the largest quantity of cupric suboxide possible, as the prob-**Necessity of saturation with CuO.** ability is then greatest that a part of the suboxide will be precipitated.   This is accomplished when cupric sulphate is carefully added to the urine, to super-saturation, i. e., the carrying out of Trommer's test exactly according to the directions given.   This depends on the following principle.

Sugar reduces more cupric oxide in a heated solution than it can in the cold.   The maximum formation of cupric suboxide and the most marked reaction is obtained when so much cupric sulphate is added that the resulting precipitate is no longer entirely dissolved by shaking, and a small quantity remains undissolved. The urine is then super-saturated to a slight degree with cupric oxide. When heated, all the cupric oxide in solution, together with the undissolved portion, will be reduced to cupric suboxide and the sugar disappears. A too great excess of copper should be avoided as this remains after heating unchanged, a dirty green cloudiness, and may, if the quantity of sugar is small, prevent the precipitation of suboxide, or at least hide it. Prolonged boiling converts the excess of copper (*Vide* 6) into a brownish-black precipitate.

9. Normal urine, to which sugar has been added, and some specimens of pathological urine may contain 0.5 per cent. of sugar and not show a precipitate of cupric suboxide when treated with Trommer's test, which precipitate alone (*Vide* 6), proves the presence of sugar. In typical diabetic urine, however, the precipitate forms when the quantity of sugar is about 0.2 per cent. Smaller quantities of sugar can therefore be detected in diabetic urine than in normal urine to which sugar has been added.

Difference between diabetic and transitory glycosuria.

This striking phenomenon is explained by the polyuria which usually exists in diabetes, the substances capable of dissolving cupric suboxide being relatively much diluted. It is accordingly often possible, in cases in which Trommer's test has not given the characteristic precipitate of cupric suboxide, to obtain this by repeating the test with another specimen of the same urine diluted with several volumes of water (*i. e.*, an artificial production of polyuria).

Another procedure which often leads to the desired reaction, is filtration through powdered animal charcoal, freed from reducing substances (sulphates, ferric protoxide salts) by treatment with sulphuric acid and water. Put some of this charcoal in a filter, and drop urine upon it until it has the consistency of paste. Make a depression in the centre into which the urine is gradually poured. Then examine the filtrate by Trommer's test. The reaction is not made more delicate by this filtration, but the precipitate of cupric suboxide can be more easily observed. The charcoal removes coloring matters, uric acid, and also small quantities of sugar, which, however, makes little difference in the qualitative analysis.

The uncertainty of Trommer's test in many cases may induce

3

the physician to discard it, and to use one of the other tests which are more reliable. This would, however, be too severe a condemnation, as Trommer's test has always this advantage for the physician, that it allows an approximate estimation of the quantity of sugar, and thereby of the severity of the case. If the reaction is easily obtained, especially by insufficient saturation with cupric oxide, the quantity of sugar is large, and the case is one of advanced diabetes. If the test succeeds only by exact saturation with cupric oxide, or if the suboxide is not precipitated, while more sensitive tests give positive results, the quantity of sugar is not more than 0.2–0.4 per cent., and the case may possibly be one of transitory glycosuria.

10. Urine containing albumin dissolves cupric oxide (Biuret reaction), but does not reduce it. Albumin does not hinder the reduction of cupric oxide, if sugar is present, but it interferes with the precipitation of cupric suboxide. Therefore, albumin in amount over 0.2 per cent. should be removed (according to Nos. 9, 4, or 11) before the test for sugar is made.

Presence of albumin.

3. *Fehling's Test.*—Fehling's solution is made by mixing together equal parts of the following solutions :

(a) 34.64 grams (534.5 grains) of pure sulphate of copper are dissolved with gentle heat in water, to which sufficient is afterwards added to make 500 c.c. (16.8 ounces). This is poured into a tightly stoppered bottle.

(b) 175 grams (2700 grains) of Rochelle salts and 100 c.c. (3⅜ ounces) of caustic soda, having a specific gravity of 1.34, are dissolved in sufficient water to make 500 c.c. (16.8 ounces), well mixed, and also kept in a well stoppered bottle.

QUALITATIVE.—If a qualitative determination alone is desired, some of the test solution is poured into a test-tube, diluted with three or four volumes of water, and boiled for a few seconds. If the solution remains clear, add a little of the suspected urine, drop by drop. The first few drops of ordinary diabetic urine will usually produce a yellow precipitate. If a volume of urine equal to that of the test solution be added, and the mixture boiled without a precipitate resulting, sugar is absent.

If a precipitate results on boiling the test solution alone, a little more soda should be added, and the fluid filtered, after which it may be again used. It is better, however, to make up a fresh solution, when an accurate analysis is desired.

QUANTITATIVE.—The principle upon which this test is based depends upon the fact that grape sugar possesses the property of reducing cupric oxide in alkaline solution, and that, when all the copper is reduced, the solution loses its blue color. The decolorization of a fixed quantity of Fehling's solution by a known quantity of urine allows the quantity of sugar contained in the urine to be readily calculated, as 10 c. c. of Fehling's solution is reduced by .05 gram of glucose.

PROCEDURE.—A known quantity of urine is diluted with 5 to 10 volumes of water. Ten c.c. of Fehling's solution are mixed with 40 c.c. of water, placed in a porcelain dish and boiled. The diluted urine is slowly added with a pipette, or, preferably, from a burette, to the diluted Fehling's solution, kept heated, until a red or yellow precipitate falls, and the fluid loses its blue color. When this exact point is reached, sufficient sugar (.05 gram) has been added to reduce the copper. From the quantity of urine required to produce this decolorization, the percentage of sugar contained in the urine can be readily calculated ; 1 c.c. = 5 per cent., 5 c.c. = 1 per cent., etc. It is often very difficult to know exactly when sufficient urine has been added. The precipitate should at times be allowed to settle, and the color of the supernatant fluid noted. If it is bluish, some copper remains undissolved ; if brownish, too much urine has been added. The test should then be repeated with greater care, but in spite of every precaution the difficulty often remains.

4. *Worm-Müller's Test (Modified Trommer's Test).—* REAGENTS NECESSARY :

(a) Aqueous solution of cupric sulphate (2.5 per cent.).

(b) Solution of 10 grams (154 grains) of pure neutral tartrate of soda and potash in 100 c.c. (3⅜ ounces) of normal solution of caustic soda (NaOH, 4 per cent.).

PROCEDURE.—5 c.c. (1¼ drachms) of urine are heated in a test-tube to the boiling point, and at the same time a mixture of 2.5 c.c. (40 minims) of solution (b), and 1 to 2 c.c. (15 to 30 minims) of solution (a) are boiled in another test-tube. Usually 1.5 grams of solution (a) are used. If, however, the specific gravity is less than 1020, it is advisable to use only 1 c.c., if higher than 1025, 2 c.c. should be used. The boiling of both urine and reagent is discontinued at the same time, and after 20 to 25 seconds they are mixed without shaking. Immediately the mixture appears bluish-green. A change then occurs if sugar is present, on account of the precipitation of cupric suboxide hydrate, the more rapidly the more sugar present. If the quantity of sugar is 0.1 per cent., the precipitate generally appears after 4 to 5 minutes as a dirty yellow cloudiness in direct light.

A precipitate may not form when the quantity of sugar is small, as the reaction then occurs only with exact quantities of copper. The test should be repeated when the result is negative, with increasing quantities of the solution of copper (2.5, 3, 3.5, 4 c.c.), until the reaction ensues, or the liquid is no longer discolored, *i. e.,* until it remains of a greenish color, an evidence of an excess of copper. This test permits the detection of .025 per cent. grape sugar, or .05 per cent. milk sugar in urine.

Specimens of normal urine often (18 in 100) show a reaction which indicates the presence of .025 to .05 per cent. of grape sugar, and which, after the action of yeast, cannot be obtained. This reaction, therefore, can be due to no other substance than grape sugar. The reason why the other reducing substances give no reaction with this test is, besides the presence of the tartrate salt, principally the keeping of the temperature below the boiling point. To accomplish this, care must be taken to allow 20 to 25 seconds for cooling, before the fluids are mixed. The grape sugar reduces very quickly at this temperature, but the other substances do not.

5. *Nylander's Bismuth Test (Modified Böttger's Test).* PRINCIPLE OF THE REACTION.—Add to an aqueous solution of grape sugar, caustic soda and a little bismuth subnitrate $No_3Bi(OH)_2$, then boil for 1–2 minutes. The bismuth salt turns black, as the sugar attracts the oxygen from it, and is converted into a black bismuth protoxide. This reaction, discovered by Böttger is, in this form not indicative of sugar alone. The modification proposed by Nylander is more accurate and reliable, as few other substances, and these occurring rarely in the urine, give this reaction.

REAGENT.—Four grams (1 drachm) of Rochelle salts are dissolved in 100 c.c. (3⅓ ounces) of a moderately warm, 8-per-cent. solution of caustic soda ; 2 grams of bismuth subnitrate are added, and the mixture shaken. The bismuth salt is converted to bismuth hydroxide Bi (OH_3) by the caustic soda, and this is dissolved by the Rochelle salts. The reagent when cold is decanted, if necessary, from the bismuth remaining undissolved, or filtered through glass wool. It preserves its activity for some time when kept in the dark.

PROCEDURE.—Add to the urine the reagent in the ratio of 1:10 and boil for 1–3 minutes. If grape sugar is present, the bismuth hydroxide is reduced, and is converted into a black, finely-divided precipitate of bismuth protoxide, which remains suspended for some time. If the urine contains .2 or. more per cent. of sugar, the black precipitate forms after 1–2 minutes, and is so marked that the urine is entirely black. If the amount of sugar is less, it forms after prolonged boiling (3 minutes). Traces of sugar (.025 per cent.) are not recognized during the heating but are detected by the grayish-black color of the earthy phosphates, precipitated by the caustic soda. The precipitate of the phosphates in urine free from sugar is snow-white.

Fourteen of 100 specimens of normal urine treated with this reagent showed slight reactions which could not be obtained after the action of yeast. These reactions must therefore have been due to grape sugar, as no other constituent of normal urine shows, with that reagent (yeast), a reaction like sugar. Such results are obtained only when Nylander's reagent is made exactly as directed ; the caustic soda, especially, should not have a higher concentration than indicated.

Urine after the ingestion of rhubarb or senna reacts to Nylander's, but not to Trommer's test. The precipitated bismuth sinks very quickly to the bottom. The presence of large quantities of rhubarb and senna is shown by the red color of the urine upon the addition of the reagent ; smaller quantities are detected by Heller's hæmoglobin test. Urine after the administration of salol and antipyrine reacts in the same manner. It is possible that this occurs after the use of many other medicines, and therefore should be kept in mind.

Albuminous urine, when boiled with Nylander's reagent, becomes brownish-red from decomposition of the albumin and the formation of bismuth sulphide. This coloration, if the quantity of albumin is not more than .2 per cent., is reddish-brown, and readily distinguished from bismuth reduced by sugar ; if the quantity of albumin is larger, it is brownish-black, and may therefore give rise to confusion. For this reason, the albumin should first be separated according to No. 11.

The presence of ammonium carbonate (alkaline fermentation) may retard the reaction, as the caustic soda of the reagent is converted into sodium carbonate and ammonia by this salt. The ammonia volatilizes immediately when boiled, and cannot therefore maintain the strong alkalinity necessary for the reduction.

6. *Phenyl-Hydrazin Test.*—Heat 10 c.c. (2½ drachms) of urine with 0.5 c.c. (7½ grains) of hydrochlorate of phenyl-hydrazin and 1.0 c.c. (15 grains) of acetate of soda for ½ hour on a water bath. If sugar is present, a precipitate of fine yellow needles, a combination of phenyl-hydrazin and grape sugar (phenyl-glucosazon), forms immediately on cooling or after a few seconds. The precipitate should be abundant (the upper part of the test-tube filled or the fluid cloudy), and macroscopically, or at least microscopically, recognizable as formed for the most part of yellow needles arranged in clusters (Fig. 5).[1]

7. *Fermentation Test.*—Saccharine urine is fermented by yeast, and the sugar converted into alcohol and carbonic-acid gas; $C_6H_{12}O_6 = 2C_2H_6O + 2CO_2$. The alcohol remains dissolved in the urine, the carbonic-acid gas escapes, but can be collected, and its bulk indicates the quantity of sugar present.

As no other normal or pathological constituent of the urine gives a similar reaction with yeast, this test is accurate and also sufficiently delicate (to 0.1 per cent. of sugar). The fact that the yeast can itself evolve carbonic-acid gas, and also that it is not always active, necessitates a control-test. Furthermore, the result is known only after some time. This test is therefore recommended if those previously mentioned have given negative results.

PROCEDURE.—This test is easily made when the fermentation tube or saccharometer (Fig. 6) is employed. Shake thoroughly together in a test-tube 10 c.c. (2.5

---

[1] For illustration, see end of volume.

drachms) of urine and 1 gram (15.4 grains) of compressed

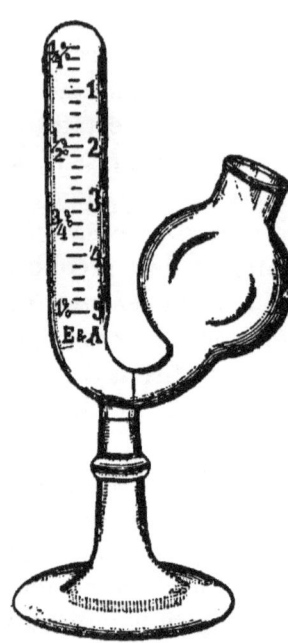

yeast (or ⅛ of a cake of Fleischman's yeast). Pour the mixture into the bulb of the saccharometer, inclining it so that the liquid will flow into the long arm, forcing out all the air. The fluid remains in the long arm due to atmospheric pressure. The tube is set aside for 12-24 hours in a room at ordinary temperature. If sugar is present, alcoholic fermentation soon begins, and carbonic-acid gas collects at the top of the long arm, driving the liquid up into the bulb. On the following day the height of the column in the long arm shows the displacement of the liquid by the gas, and the figures indicate the approximate quantity

FIG. 6.—EINHORN'S SAC-
CHAROMETER.

of sugar contained in such urine. Urine containing a large quantity of sugar should be diluted five to ten times, and the result multiplied proportionately. A control-test should be made in a similar tube with normal urine and yeast. If the control-test shows a small bubble the yeast is active. A few drops of a 10 per cent. solution of tartaric acid should be added to faintly acid or alkaline urine to prevent putrefaction, which is injurious to the test.

METHOD OF ROBERTS.—An approximate estimation can also be obtained by the determination of the specific gravity before and after alcoholic fermentation. This is based on the fact that diabetic urine undergoing fermentation loses in specific gravity. Experiment has shown that every degree in specific gravity lost in fermentation corresponds to one grain of sugar per fluid ounce. Roberts recommends the following procedure : about 4 ounces of the saccharine urine are placed in a 12-ounce bottle, and a lump of ordinary yeast about the size of a small nut is added. This bottle is then closed with a nicked cork to permit the escape of the carbonic-acid gas, and placed on a mantelpiece or other warm place. Beside it is put a tightly corked 4-ounce vial, filled with the same urine but without yeast. In 18–24 hours the fermentation will be complete. This is shown when the urine has become more transparent, the effervescence and formation of foam has ceased, and the greater part of the yeast has sunk to the bottom. It can, however, be definitely determined by its non-reaction if some of the urine, taken out with a pipette, is subjected to one of the tests for sugar. The specific gravity of the decanted fermented urine is taken and also that of the unfermented urine. If the unfermented urine has a specific gravity of 1030 and the fermented urine 1020, then the urine contains 10 grains of sugar to the fluid ounce.

It is advisable in all cases not entirely clear, in spite of the positive result in the reducing tests, to determine the presence of grape sugar by the fermentation test.

8. *Indigo Test.*—Add to an aqueous solution of grape sugar, rendered strongly alkaline with carbonate of soda, a solution of indigo carmine (indigo sulphate) until the solution is distinctly blue, then boil. The color changes to yellow, and becomes blue again when shaken up with air. The indigo carmine is reduced by the sugar, and is then oxidized to indigo blue by the oxygen of the air.

This test is neither especially sensitive nor characteristic of grape sugar in urine. The test papers, sold for the detection of sugar in urine, depend on this reaction. They consist of strips of paper, some of which have been saturated with a solution of indigo carmine, others with a solution of soda and then dried. Place a strip of the indigo paper in water, add this blue solution to the urine until it has a faintly blue color, then put in the fluid a large strip of the soda paper and boil. If sugar is present the change in color as above occurs.

21. GLYCURONIC ACID $(C_6H_{10}O_7)$.—Its presence is ordinarily of little clinical importance, but as it may be mistaken for sugar, since it reacts in the same manner, its occurrence should be kept in mind. Normally it occurs in such small quantities that it may be disregarded, but after the ingestion of certain substances, as camphor, turpentine, kairin, nitro-toluol, chloral, chloroform, its quantity may be so greatly increased as to lead to error. In such cases the fermentation test, which is not affected by the presence of glycuronic acid, should be employed.

22. ACETONE $(CH_3-CO-CH_3)$.—A volatile fluid having an ethereal odor usually present in urine when the consumption of albumin is increased (diabetes, fever, meat diet, and starvation in health).

1. *Legal's Test.*—Add to urine (one drachm), 2 or 3 drops of a freshly prepared concentrated solution of nitro-prussic soda and a few drops of caustic soda. The urine becomes purplish-red, and after a few minutes changes to a yellow color. Now let a few drops of concentrated acetic acid carefully flow upon it without mixing. If acetone is present, the junction of the fluids has a carmine or purplish-red color, and after some hours becomes a dirty bluish-green, due to the formation of Prussian blue. The characteristic of this test is not the red coloration in alkaline solution, as a constituent of normal urine (kreatinin) shows this reaction, but the change to red on the addition of acetic acid.

2. *Lieben's Iodoform Test.*—Two grams (30 grains) of potassium iodide are dissolved in 6 c. c. (1.5 drachms) of liquor potassæ and the solution boiled. The urine is carefully placed on the surface of this solution in a test-tube. At the plane of contact a precipitation of phosphates occurs. This becomes yellow and shows crystals of iodoform if acetone is present. The test is much more certain when applied to a distillate of the urine made by evaporating urine to which a small quantity of phosphoric acid has been added.

23. Di-Acetic Acid (CH_3CO-CH_2COOH).—It is very easily converted into acetone and carbonic-acid gas. It reacts to Legal's test like acetone, and in aqueous or ethereal solutions changes on addition of solution of ferric chloride to a dark-red, which disappears after a time when an acid has been added (Gerhardt's reaction).

Di-acetic acid is present in the urine of most of the severe cases of diabetes (always in diabetic coma), very rarely in high fevers and nervous disorders of adults, more often in those of children.

Determination of its Presence.—Add to urine 1–2 drops of liquor ferri chloridi, separate by filtration the yellowish-white precipitate of iron phosphate, and add to the filtrate more of the solution of iron. If a violet to a dark-red coloration appears, the presence of di-acetic acid is probable. Rhodan oxide, formic acid, acetic acid, salicylic acid, the products of kairin, thallin, antipyrin, etc., form combinations with iron showing the same color reaction. Two control-tests, with a fresh specimen of urine, should be made to determine absolutely its presence. Boil one portion of the urine, and when cold add the solution of iron as above. The red coloration should not appear, since the di-acetic acid is destroyed by boiling. Acidulate the other portion with diluted sulphuric acid, extract with ether, and add a few drops of the solution of iron. If the ether assumes a dark-red color, which disappears after forty-eight hours at the longest, di-acetic acid is present. The di-acetic acid is in this test freed from its salts by the sulphuric acid and passes into the ether.

24. FAT.—Small quantities of fat may appear in the urine after the consumption of an excess of oleaginous food, in Bright's disease with a fatty degeneration of the kidney, in cases of prolonged suppuration, phthisis, and pyæmia, in diabetes mellitus, and in phosphorus poisoning. Its presence is easily detected by shaking the turbid urine with ether, which dissolves the fat and thus clarifies the urine. The fat globules may also be recognized by microscopic examination from their highly refractive character.

CHYLE, which consists of lymph cells and fat globules in a state of minute subdivision, has been found in the urine in a disease termed chyluria, seen almost exclusively in the tropics and due to the presence of a parasite, filaria sanguinis hominis. It gives to the urine a milky appearance.

25. UREA $CO(NH_2)_2$.—Urea is the most important of the products of nitrogenous metabolism, the substances excreted from the body, and of which nitrogen forms a constituent. The quantity of urea eliminated by a healthy adult in twenty-four hours ranges from 32–40 grms. (493 to 616 grains), but it varies greatly within physiological limits, and much more in morbid conditions.

The chief cause of this variation in health is the character of the food ingested. If the diet contains few proteids it may sink to from 15–20 grms. (231–308.6 grains). If it is rich in proteids it may reach

100 grms. (1543 grains) in twenty-four hours. In disease its excretion is increased in fevers, diabetes mellitus, diminished in diseases of the liver, and in chronic diseases characterized by malnutrition, and may entirely cease in uræmia. Its quantity is as a rule an indication of the state of tissue metabolism, and therefore of great clinical value. A positive deduction in regard to tissue metabolism can only be made from its quantity when the quantity of nitrogenous compounds ingested with the food, and the quantity eliminated by other channels, the bowel, the skin, and the lungs, are considered.

HYPOBROMITE METHOD.—An approximate estimate of the quantity of urea is easily determined by this method with the apparatus designed by Doremus (Fig. 7).

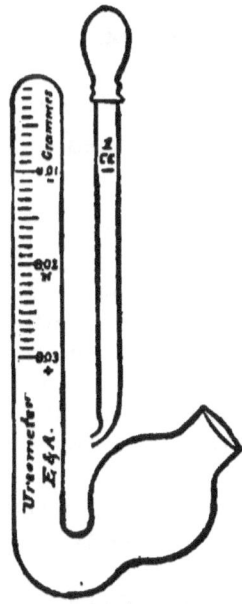

This method is based upon the fact that when urea is oxidized in a strongly alkaline medium, the nitrogen alone remains uncombined. The quantity of nitrogen evolved indicates the quantity of urea. as 1 c.c. of nitrogen = .0027 grm. urea.

Fill the long arm and curve of the ureometer with the hypobromite solution, diluted with an equal volume of water. Draw up into the pipette 1 c.c. of urine (to the mark), pass the pipette well into the long arm as far as possible and compress the nipple gently and steadily, forcing all the urine into the hypobromite solution, but taking care not to drive any air after the urine. When the decomposition is complete, as shown by a cessation of the effervescence, the quantity of urea can be read off from the scale.

FIG. 7.—DOREMUS' UREOMETER.

The hypobromite solution is made by dissolving 100 grams (1543 grains) of caustic soda in 250 c.c. (8.6 ounces) of water, allowing it to cool and adding 25 c.c. (6¾ drachms) of bromine. It is advisable to make up only a small quantity when required as the solution does not keep. A mixture of the urine of twenty-four hours should be examined as the quantity of urea varies markedly at different times in the day.

An approximate estimate of the quantity of urea usually sufficiently accurate for clinical purposes can be made from the specific gravity of a mixture of all the urine excreted in twenty-four hours in almost all cases except those of diabetes mellitus. Forty-six hundredths of the total solids determined by multiplying the last two figures of the specific gravity by 2.33 (Haser's coefficient) will approximately be the quantity of urea in grams in 1000 c.c. of urine.

If the urine contains a large quantity of urea, large crystals of urea, often visible macroscopically, are formed on the addition of nitric acid.

26. URIC ACID ($C_5H_4N_4O_3$). Uric acid is also a product of nitrogenous metabolism, and is excreted, combined with sodium and potassium, in the urine of a healthy adult in quantity varying from 0.5–.75 grams (7.5–10 grains) every twenty-four hours.

It is increased in health by an abundant meat diet and in disease as fevers, leukæmia, pernicious anæmia, and affections of the heart and lungs characterized by dyspnœa. It is diminished in a number of chronic diseases ; nephritis, arthritis, diabetes, and especially in gout after the acute paroxysm. Certain nervous conditions, neurasthenia, migraine, chorea, etc., are said by Herter[1] to be distinguished by an increase in the ratio of uric acid to urea.

Its presence, when free, is easily recognized by microscopic examination, as the crystals have characteristic shapes and are always yellowish-red in color (Fig. 9).

Murexide Test.—Dissolve a little of the urinary sediment with a few drops of concentrated nitric acid in a porcelain dish by heat and evaporate carefully to dryness.

---

[1] " The Excretion of Uric Acid," *N. Y. Med. Journal*, June 4, 1892.

A yellow or reddish-yellow flake remains which when moistened with a trace of ammonia becomes a rich purple red, with caustic soda or potash a beautiful violet or blue. They are distinguished from xanthin and guanin by the disappearance of the color when heated.

QUANTITATIVE ESTIMATION, HEINTZ' METHOD.—Add 5 c.c. (1⅓ drachms) of hydrochloric acid to 100 c.c. (3.3 ounces) of urine. Set the mixture aside for twenty-four hours, then collect the crystals on a weighed filter-paper, wash with diluted hydrochloric. acid, dry at 100° C. and weigh. The increase in weight is the percentage of urea. In some cases however no precipitate is obtained by this method.

The other methods are so tedious and complicated as to be of little clinical value.

III.—Inorganic Substances.

27. SULPHURETTED HYDROGEN (H_2S).—The common cause of hydrothionuria is the decomposition of those normal constituents of the urine which contain sulphur, due to special bacteria in the urinary tract (cystitis, pyelitis).

If the urine when voided shows neither indication of fermentation nor cloudiness due to bacteria, an extraneous cause is to be thought of (contamination from air, pus, or the intestines). Urine is suitable for examination only when recently voided, as sulphuretted hydrogen may be present on account of fermentation in any specimen of urine after standing, or if brought from a distance it may have been destroyed when present by oxidation.

PROCEDURE.—A current of air is forced through the urine and directed by means of a small, narrow glass tube against a strip of paper saturated with lead acetate and ammonia. If sulphuretted hydrogen is present, the paper becomes brown or black in a few minutes. This coloration is due to the formation of lead sulphide. The principle is the reverse of that of the syphon. Air should not be blown through for more than ten minutes, as in such cases H_2S may be formed in urine which did not originally contain it.

If sulphuretted hydrogen is present in large quantity, the paper may be fastened in the neck of the bottle by means of the cork. The strip of paper becomes brown, at least at the edge, after the bottle has been repeatedly shaken and allowed to stand for a few minutes. Strips of filtering paper saturated with a solution of acetate of lead should be kept in stock and moistened with ammonia before use.

28. THE CHLORIDES.—The principal chloride found in the urine is sodium chloride, of which 10–13 grams (154–200 grains) are excreted daily. Potassium, ammonium, and magnesium chlorides are also present, but in small quantities.

The amount of the chlorides varies with the quantity of salt contained in the food ingested and also in certain diseases. It is markedly diminished in acute febrile conditions and is almost entirely absent in croupous pneumonia, its reappearance indicating improvement. It is increased in diabetes and in some forms of nephritis with polyuria.

DETERMINATION.—Acidulate the urine strongly with nitric acid and add a few drops of a solution of nitrate of silver. If the chlorides are abundant a heavy white precipitate of chloride of silver forms, if present in small amount only a milky cloudiness appears. Other silver salts, especially the phosphate of silver, are dissolved by the nitric acid.

29. THE SULPHATES.—They appear in urine as simple sulphates of potassium, sodium, magnesium, and calcium, and as ethereal sulphates. Their amount varies from 1.5–3 grams (23–46 grains), depending upon the food taken, but more especially upon the metabolism of the proteids. Little clinical value can be placed upon an increase or decrease of the sulphates in disease.

DETERMINATION.—Acidulate the urine, which is first filtered, with acetic acid and add a solution of barium chloride. A white precipitate of barium sulphate results.

30. THE PHOSPHATES.—They are found in the urine as alkaline phosphates (sodium, potassium, and ammonium) and as earthy phosphate (calcium and magnesium).

As phosphoric acid is tri-basic, it forms three classes of salts—an acid, a neutral, and a basic salt. The alkaline phosphates are soluble in water while the earthy phosphates vary in their degree of solubility, the acid (mono-) phosphates being soluble, the neutral (di-) phosphates with difficulty soluble, and the basic (tri-) phosphates almost insoluble (see page 10). The quantity of phosphoric acid excreted in the urine daily ranges from 2–3 grams (31–46 grains). It is increased in inflammations of the brain, phthisis, and leukæmia ; diminished in gout, in most acute diseases, in disease of the kidney, during pregnancy, and in rachitis.

DETERMINATION.—Render the urine alkaline with caustic potash or ammonia and gently heat. A flaky precipitate of earthy phosphates results.

To detect the alkaline phosphates, treat the urine with ammonia, then filter. Add to the filtrate a mixture of the sulphates of magnesia and ammonia which precipitate the phosphates as triple phosphates.

31. THE CARBONATES.—The carbonate of soda, lime, magnesia, and ammonia are usually present in alkaline urine.

They are formed from the carbonates of the food, also from the citrates, malates, and tartrates converted into carbonates in the organism. They are therefore more abundant with a vegetable diet. The ammonia salt however when found in large quantity is due to alkaline fermentation. Urine containing carbonates is either cloudy when passed or soon becomes turbid on standing.

DETERMINATION.—Urine containing carbonates when treated with an acid, evolves a colorless gas which renders baryta water turbid.

As the quantities of the inorganic constituents of the urine depend to a very great extent upon the character of the food ingested, quantitative tests, which are tedious and complicated, are of clinical value only when the quantities of such substances contained in the ingesta and absorbed are known.

IV.—Accidental Constituents.

32. MERCURY.—Acidulate 250 c.c. (8.5 ounces) of urine with 5 c.c. (1¼ drachms) of diluted hydrochloric acid, then add some strips of tinsel, which are acted upon for an hour at a temperature of 60°–80° C. (140°–176° F.). The tinsel is then removed, washed with water, alcohol, and ether, dried, placed in a long, narrow, dry glass tube, and heated to a dull red heat. The mercury, which has formed an amalgam with the tinsel, is volatilized, and condenses on the cooler part of the tube in microscopically small globules. If after cooling a grain of iodine is placed in the tube, it is volatilized by gentle heat, and small red crystals, as if spattered, become visible, due to the formation of red iodide of mercury. 1 : 10,000 can be detected by this method.

33. CHLORATE OF POTASSIUM.—Heat the urine with ¼ its volume of concentrated hydrochloric acid. The

urine assumes first a reddish to violet coloration, due to
the decomposition of the indican by the hydrochloric
acid, then, if chloric acid is present, it becomes either
yellowish or colorless.

One part in 10,000 may be detected by this reaction. The chloric
acid is freed by the hydrochloric acid and converted into chlorine,
part of which acts on the pigment of the urine, and part escapes as
gas, which may be detected if in any quantity by its odor and by its
action on a piece of litmus-paper held in the mouth of the test-tube.

34. IODOFORM, IODINE, IODIDES.—1. Add to urine a
few drops of starch-paste (1 part of starch boiled with
30–50 of water), and pour this carefully on concentrated, yellow nitric acid. If iodine is present, a transitory, deep-blue ring appears at the junction of the
fluids.

One part in 100,000 can be detected in this manner. It is therefore employed as a test of the absorbent power of the stomach, as the
iodides can be given in small doses, 0.1–0.2 grams (1½–3 grains).

2. Add to urine 5–10 drops of concentrated, yellow
nitric acid, and shake the mixture with 1–2 c.c. (10–20
minims) of chloroform. If iodine is present, the chloroform, which has sunk to the bottom, assumes a beautiful
violet color. This is more sensitive than the previous
reaction. Iodine, in both tests, is set free from its salts
by the nitrous di-oxide, contained in the yellow nitric
acid, and dissolves in the chloroform in the one, or
unites with the starch in the other. Other oxidizing
agents, chlorine water or hypo-chloride of calcium, may
be employed in place of the nitric acid.

35. BROMINE SALTS.—Add to urine either a few
drops of a solution of hypo-chlorite of calcium and

hydrochloric acid or chlorine water, then shake the mixture with 1 c.c. (10 minims) of chloroform. If bromine is present, the chloroform assumes a yellow coloration. Not less than 0.1 per cent. of potassium, sodium, or ammonium bromide can be determined.

36. CARBOLIC ACID.—The urine is of a dark-green color when voided, and becomes black on standing. It does not react to the common tests for carbolic acid, as the carbolic acid in the urine is combined.

37. SALICYLIC ACID, SALOL, SALICYLURIC ACID.— Add to urine a few drops of a solution of ferric chloride, if the urine is normal, a heavy, yellow precipitate of iron phosphate forms, if salicylic acid is present, it assumes an intensely violet coloration (compare 23, di-acetic acid). If the quantity is very small (1 : 12,000), acidulate the urine with hydrochloric acid, and shake with ether, in which, diluted with water, the reaction will appear on the addition of the solution of iron.

These substances may be employed to determine gastric absorption in the same manner as iodide of potassium, because of their easy detection and innocuousness in small doses.

This reaction occurs only if the solution of ferric chloride is neutral, as free hydrochloric acid decomposes the salicylate of iron. Phenol acts in the same manner.

38. TANNIN (DI-GALLIC ACID).—It appears in the urine partly as gallic acid. Both acids, when treated with solution of ferric chloride, assume a dark-blue or a bluish-black coloration, with alkalies they become brown, due to their oxidation.

39. CHRYSOPHANIC ACID.—It appears in the urine after the administration of chrysarobin, rhubarb, or senna. Alkalies color such urine red, and lime-salts

form a red precipitate. Differentiate it by means of ether from the pigment after the use of santonin, which acts in a similar manner. The chrysophanic acid passes into the ether, and gives a red coloration to it on the addition of caustic soda.

40. BALSAM OF COPAIBA.—After its use the line of polarization is deflected to the left, and the urine can reduce cupric oxide, but not bismuth oxide. When a mineral acid is added, it becomes cloudy from the precipitation of resinous acids, and immediately assumes a purplish-red, then a violet color. Heat and an oxidizing agent, *e. g.* hypo-chlorite of calcium, produce this reaction.

41. ALKALOIDS.—These form with acetic acid and the solution of potassio-mercuric iodide precipitates distinguished from albumin, peptone, and mucus by their solubility in alcohol. The detection of the different alkaloids requires more complicated methods than can be given here.

V.—Urinary Deposits.

The urinary deposits may be either unorganized, chemical substances, as uric acid, urates, phosphates, etc., or organized, anatomical elements, as blood cells, mucus, casts, etc. The methods for their examination are chemical, microscopical, and micro-chemical. The deposits are obtained in several ways.

42.—1. If the urine has been standing, pour off the clear supernatant fluid and allow the remainder to settle for twelve hours in a conical glass or test-tube. Remove a little of the sediment with a pipette, introducing it with its upper opening closed by the forefinger into the sediment, then raise the finger, allowing some of the sediment to enter the tube and replace the finger on its removal. Allow the urine on the outside to run off, and, by moving the finger, place the desired amount of sediment on a slide, cover with a glass, and examine under a microscope.

2. If an immediate examination of the sediment is desired for diagnosis, or if an earlier examination on account of the rapid decomposition of urine in summer[1] is necessary, a deposit of the sediment may be quickly produced by the use of the Litten centrifugal machine[2] (Fig. 8). Test-tubes made of glass thicker than usual and with c o n i c a l bottoms should be used. They are f i l l e d with urine, placed in the holders, and rotated for three minutes. All the sediment is thrown to the bottom, and usually appears as a turbidity or dense crust.

FIG. 8.—THE LITTEN CENTRIFUGAL MACHINE.

3. Another method for rapidly obtaining the sediment is by electrolysis.[3] Pieces of iron wire are attached to

---

[1] Otherwise the urine should be treated with an antiseptic, thymol or salicylic acid, and kept in a cool place.

[2] Sold by J. T. Dougherty, 411 West Fifty-ninth Street, New York City.

[3] *Centralblatt für klinische Medicin,* January 7, 1893.

the poles of a battery, consisting of two zinc-carbon elements, and inserted some distance apart through the cork bottom of a cylinder filled with urine. The oxygen and hydrogen from the decomposition of water, which is continued for five to ten minutes, carry up, as they arise, all the sediment of the urine and this is held in the foam at the top of the column of urine. A little of the lower surface of the foam, where the urinary constituents are held, should be removed with a pipette. This method has not given results as satisfactory as either of the other methods.

I.—UNORGANIZED SEDIMENT.

A.—SEDIMENT OF ACID URINE.

43. URIC ACID.—Uric acid occurs in crystals of a reddish-yellow or reddish-brown color, due to the urinary pigment. The crystals vary in shape and size, and can often be recognized by the unaided eye as sand, gravel, etc. The basis-shape is the rhombic plate, which may become hexagonal, or most commonly elliptic, like a whetstone. They may also resemble rosettes, sections of a barrel, balls, and crystals of the most irregular shape, with striated spicules (Fig. 9)—all characterized by their color, and by it alone readily recognized. The very irregular crystals are due to the rapid precipitation of uric acid, especially where there is a great tendency to concentration of urine and therefore a predisposition to the formation of stone.

44. URATES.—A yellow- or brick-red amorphous sediment (sedimentum lateritium), which often adheres strongly to the vessel, consists of the acid urates (urates

of the general formula, $C_5 H_3 N_4 O_3 M$), principally urates of soda, and usually also of some uric acid. It is characterized by its complete solubility when the urine is warmed. The urates appear under the microscope as fine granules, in heaps or like moss, and reflect no color.

CHEMICAL REACTION OF URIC ACID AND URATES.

1. The urates are readily dissolved by heat, even before the solution boils.

FIG. 9.—URIC-ACID CRYSTALS.

2. The urates are dissolved on the addition of acetic acid, and large crystals of uric acid (usually quadratic or rhombic plates) appear after a time in their place.

3. Uric acid is dissolved slowly in warm water, rapidly even in the cold, on the addition of alkalies (caustic soda).

4. Urates and uric acid react to the murexide test (Art. 26).

45. OXALATE OF LIME, CaC_2O_4.—These crystals have been found in small quantity in normal urine. Their number, however, is often markedly increased after the ingestion of tomatoes, asparagus, beet root, fresh beans, etc., vegetables containing much oxalic acid, and in conditions of mal-nutrition.

They settle very slowly on account of their lightness, and are therefore often overlooked.

MICROSCOPICAL APPEARANCE.—They appear in two forms.

1. Transparent, strongly refracting octahedral crystals (envelope shape), less often short or long prisms with pyramidal ends, (combination of the octahedral shape and the prism, Fig. 10). The perfect octahedral crystals are characteristic of calcium oxalate; the other shapes may be confounded with ammonio-magnesium phosphate.

FIG. 10.—CALCIUM-OXALATE CRYSTALS.

2. Round or oval disks, having a central contracture (sand-clock, dumb-bell, or spheroid shape; Fig. 10). These unusual shapes are not characteristic, and may be confused with calcium carbonate, uric acid, or ammonium urate.

CHEMICAL REACTION. — Insoluble in acetic acid, readily soluble in mineral acids (hydrochloric acid).

B.—SEDIMENT OF SLIGHTLY ACID (AMPHOTERIC) URINE.

46. DI-CALCIUM PHOSPHATE (neutral phosphate of lime, $CaHPO_4 + 2 H_2O$).—An uncommon sediment. Wedge-shaped crystals, arranged in the form of

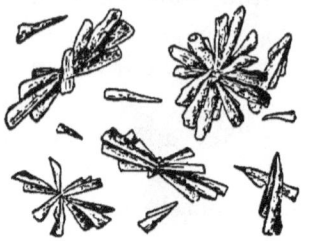

sheaves or rosettes, Fig. 11. They are often very small, and so crowded together that their structure is recognized with difficulty. Decomposed by ammonia, and very soluble in acetic acid.

FIG. 11.—DI-CALCIUM-PHOSPHATE CRYSTALS (JAKSCH).

47. AMMONIO-MAGNESIUM PHOSPHATES.—(*Vide* 49.)

C.—SEDIMENT OF ALKALINE URINE.

48. EARTHY PHOSPHATES.—Tri-calcium and tri-magnesium phosphates, $Ca_3 (PO_4)_2$ and $Mg_3 (PO_4)_2$. Small amorphous granules occurring singly or in transparent, ill-defined groups. Very soluble in acetic acid.

49. AMMONIO-MAGNESIUM PHOSPHATE (triple phosphates, $NH_4Mg PO_4 + 6 H_2O$).—Large three-, four-, or six-sided prisms,

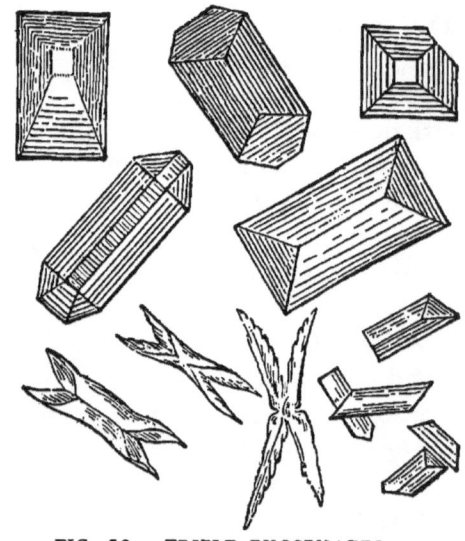

FIG. 12.—TRIPLE PHOSPHATES.

with bevelled ends (coffin-lid shape) ; they may, however, exhibit very irregular shapes and have jagged edges (Fig. 12). A common sediment in alkaline urine, readily soluble in acetic acid.

50. AMMONIUM URATES. — Large, usually dark-yellow, spherical bodies, singly or in groups, and usually beset with radiating spicules (thorn-apple shape); rarely large balls (Fig. 13).

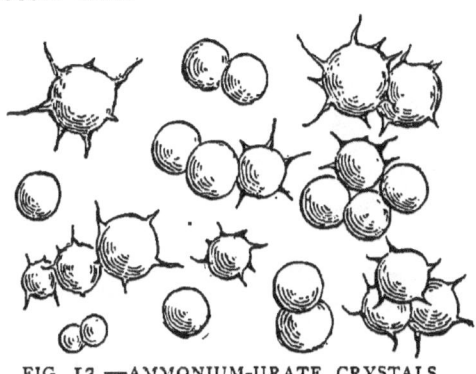

FIG. 13.—AMMONIUM-URATE CRYSTALS.

A common sediment in alkaline fermentation, soluble in acetic acid, with the formation of crystals of uric acid ; soluble with difficulty in water.

OXALATE OF CALCIUM (*vide* 45) and other constituents of acid urine (uric acid, urates) may be found if the reaction becomes alkaline after their precipitation. Such sediment persists for a long time when enclosed in mucus, which retards the equalization of the reaction.

D.—UNCOMMON URINARY DEPOSIT.

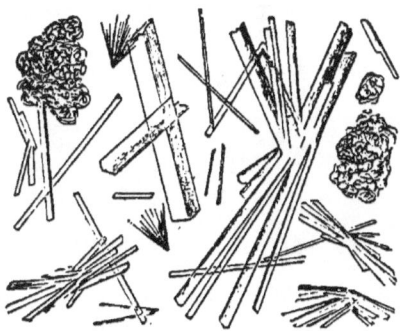

51. SULPHATE OF CALCIUM, $CaSO_4 + 2 H_2O$.—Long prisms or plates, with sharply cut ends, singly or in groups (Fig. 14). Insoluble in acetic acid, soluble with difficulty in mineral acids and

FIG. 14.—CALCIUM SULPHATE (JAKSCH). in water.

52. CARBONATE OF CALCIUM, Ca Co$_3$.—Amorphous or crystallized in groups of granules or small iridescent flakes on the surface of the urine (Fig. 15).

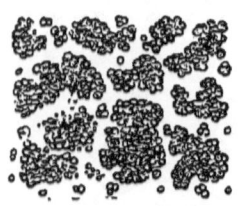

FIG. 15.—CALCIUM CARBONATE (JAKSCH).

Very soluble in acetic acid with the evolution of carbonic-acid gas. The normal sediment in the urine of vegetarians.

53. CRYSTALLINE TRI-MAGNESIUM PHOSPHATE, Mg$_3$ (PO$_4$)$_2$ + 22 H$_2$O.—Long, smooth, strongly refracting, rhomboidal plates, very soluble in acetic acid.

54. CYSTIN.—Colorless, symmetrical hexagonal plates. Insoluble in acetic acid, soluble in mineral acids, alkalies, and also in ammonia, which distinguishes it from uric acid.

55. LEUCIN AND TYROSIN.—Often present in acute yellow atrophy of the liver and in phosphorus poisoning; seldom in severe cases of typhoid fever, variola, and pernicious anæmia.

LEUCIN is moderately soluble in water, and crystallizes, when pure, in delicate flakes; when impure, in balls and amorphous masses, formed of groups of flakes (Fig. 16). They are

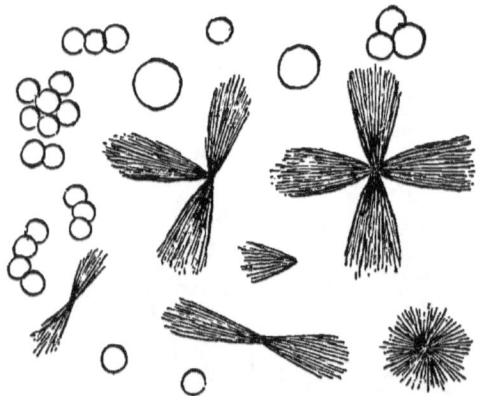

FIG. 16.—LEUCIN AND TYROSIN.

distinguished from fat by their inferior light refraction and their insolubility in ether, from ammonium urate by their action with acids.

TYROSIN is with difficulty soluble in cold water, but is more soluble in acids and alkalies. It crystallizes in tufts, sheaves, or balls, formed of very fine needles (Fig. 16), and assumes a beautiful red coloration when heated with Millon's reagent (a mixture of equal parts of mercury and nitric acid, diluted with twice its bulk of water and then after some hours separated by filtration from the precipitate formed).

Leucin very rarely, tyrosin seldom, appears as a sediment in urine. Either, however, may in most cases be obtained if the urine is concentrated by heat, or treated with acetate of lead, and the filtrate freed from lead by sulphuretted hydrogen and concentrated. The precipitate is recognized by its microscopic and chemical character.

56. HIPPURIC ACID.—The crystals have the form of needles or rhomboidal prisms (Fig. 17). They may be confounded with ammonio - magnesium phosphate or uric acid ; from the former they are distinguished by their insolubility in acetic acid, from the latter by the failure of the murexide test.

FIG. 17.—HIPPURIC ACID (JAKSCH).

57. BILIRUBIN.—Amorphous yellow granules, needles, or plates, found in pus-cells or fat globules. Soluble in caustic soda.

58. HÆMOGLOBIN.—Amorphous or crystalline found in casts.

59. FAT.—Strongly refracting globules of varying

size, readily soluble in ether. Gives off an odor like acrolein (acrylic aldehyde) when heated on a platinum foil.

In lipuria fat alone is present, in chyluria albumin is also found in the urine. They are by this difference easily distinguished from each other.

2.—ORGANIZED SEDIMENT.

60. Mucus.—It occurs normally in urine partly dissolved and partly as a marked turbidity which sinks to the bottom as a heavy cloud, but in catarrhal conditions of the urinary passages its quantity is greatly increased. Under the microscope it is transparent, and recognized only by the elements embedded in it (urates, epithelial cells, leucocytes, etc.). The ribbon-shaped mucous threads have a distant resemblance to urinary casts. The addition of diluted acetic acid to mucus produces a flocculent precipitate, not soluble in an excess of the acid, or on application of heat. Mucus disappears almost completely on the addition of caustic soda. This reaction distinguishes it from pus.

61. Pus (Leucocytes).—A few leucocytes, granular masses of protoplasm with nuclei, may be present in normal urine, but an increased quantity indicates a suppurative condition of some part of the urinary tract, as urethritis, cystitis, pyelitis, abscess, tuberculosis. In women, however, pus found in the urine may be derived from the vaginal secretion. If pus is present in any quantity, a yellowish sediment forms. Leucocytes can generally be recognized by the microscope (Fig. 18) ; in acid or neutral urine they preserve their form, while in alkaline urine (alkaline fermentation) they swell up into

a formless, glairy mass, due to the action of the ammonia. The addition of iodo-potassic-iodide solution distin-

guishes them from forms of epithelial cells when there is doubt, the leucocytes becoming a deep mahogany-brown, the epithelial cells a light yellow. The addition of 1 per cent. acetic acid is usually necessary to make visible the nuclei. If liquor potassæ is added to a de-

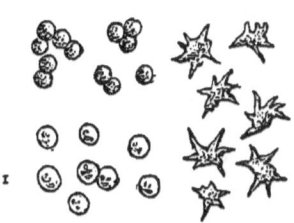

FIG. 18.—LEUCOCYTES.
1, Leucocytes treated with acetic acid.

posit of pus, it is converted into a viscid gelatinous mass (Donne's test). Urine containing pus always exhibits the reactions for albumin.

62. RED BLOOD CELLS.—They are found as a morbid element in the urine, and may vary in quantity from a

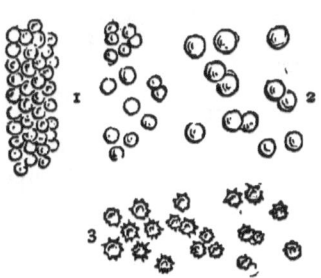

FIG. 19.—RED BLOOD CELLS.
1, Normal blood cells ; 2, swollen blood cells ; 3, shrunken blood cells.

few cells seen with difficulty by the microscope to a mass easily recognized by the unaided eye. In fresh acid urine they are of normal size, shape and color, but they soon undergo a change, becoming either larger and swollen or contracted and crenated. They never take on an appearance like that of a roll of coins (Fig. 19). After a time they lose their sharp, regular outline, and in ammoniacal urine are soon dissolved (see page 19).

63. EPITHELIAL CELLS.—They occur in small num-

bers in normal urine, but are much increased in numbers in certain pathological conditions—irritation or inflammation of any part of the urinary tract. They are masses of protoplasm, larger than leucocytes, having single nuclei, visible without treatment with acetic acid, and more or less granular in structure (Fig. 20). They have at times been confounded with leucocytes, but their polygonal shape and single, large, round, or oval nucleus usually renders the differentiation easy. Though their shape is characteristic of the part of the urinary

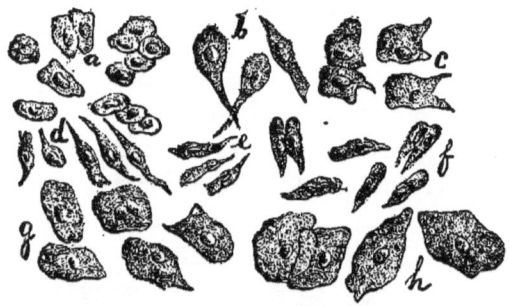

FIG. 20.—EPITHELIAL CELLS.

From (a) the uriniferous tubules, (b) the pelvis, (c) the bladder, (d) the ureter, (e) the prostate, (f) the male urethra, (g) female urethra, (h) vagina.

tract from which they come, it is usually difficult to determine exactly their origin, as many are very similar, and the appearance of others may be much affected by maceration in the urine. The following shapes are easily distinguished :

Origin.

1. Round—Uriniferous tubules.
2. Caudate—Pelvis of the kidney, ureter, male urethra.
3. Large polygonal—Bladder, female urethra, vagina.

64. CASTS.—These are moulds of renal tubules, and occur in the urine, with a few exceptions, only in disease of the kidney and with albuminous urine. They are formed from proteids coagulated in the tubules, the proteids having been allowed to pass from the blood into the tubules on account of a morbid condition of the epithelial cells. These moulds block up the tubules until the pressure of the urine from behind is sufficient to carry them out into the urine. They are divided into :

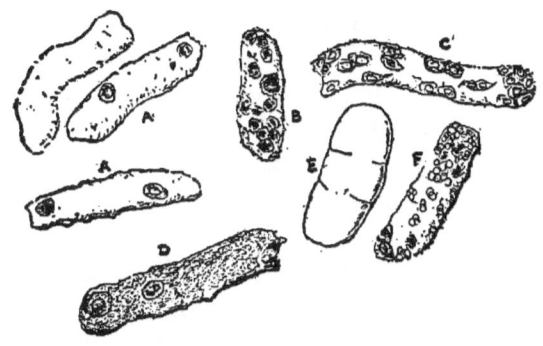

FIG. 21.—CASTS.

A, Hyaline casts ; B, hyaline casts with leucocytes ; C, epithelial cast ; D, granular cast ; E, waxy cast ; F, blood cast.

a. EPITHELIAL CASTS.—Produced by the coagulation of blood plasma, which has escaped into the tubules. They are covered more or less completely with the degenerated epithelium (Fig. 21).

b. BLOOD CASTS.—Casts of tubes into which a hemorrhage has taken place. They may contain only entangled blood cells, or at times may seem to be formed entirely of blood cells (Figs. 19 and 21).

c. GRANULAR CASTS.—They are usually of variable

5

size and imperfect form. The granulation may be very fine, or less often somewhat coarse, and their color varies from a pale-yellow to a reddish-brown. Leucocytes, fat globules, and crystals may occasionally be seen upon them. They are probably formed from the debris of degenerated epithelial or blood cells (Fig. 21).

d. HYALINE CASTS.—Pale, transparent, almost structureless forms, detected with great difficulty. They are the coagulated products of the exudation of blood plasma into the tubules. They are of larger size when formed in tubules previously stripped of epithelium. They may also occasionally be formed from the secretion of the epithelium lining the tubules, and thus not indicate severe renal disease (Fig. 21).

e. WAXY CASTS. — Characterized by their greater length, and when short by their great breadth. Under the microscope, they appear homogeneous, strongly refractive, and often segmented. Fat globules, epithelial cells, blood cells, fungi, and various crystals may frequently be seen upon their surface. They are distinguished from hyaline casts by their strongly refractive character and their great resistance to acids. Their formation is probably due to a degeneration of the epithelium and exudation of morbid products (amyloid material, fibrin) (Fig. 21).

f. URATE CASTS.—Crystals of urate of soda may assume the form of the tubule into which they are excreted. They dissolve on the application of heat. They have been found in cases of gout and renal congestion, but do not necessarily indicate severe renal disease.

The great diagnostic importance of the presence of casts in the urine depends upon the fact that they, with a few exceptions, indicate renal disease. Hyaline casts have often been found in catarrhal icterus and also at times in the urine in cases of fever, severe anæmia, leukæmia, and diabetes without renal complication. But the presence of blood, epithelial, granular, or waxy casts, is always of serious significance. The casts are usually the more numerous the greater the quantity of albumin and the more severe the disease, although there are many exceptions to this. The casts often appear in the beginning of a nephritis before albuminuria is detected and usually in the recovery of acute nephritis continue after the albumin has disappeared.

It at times happens that casts are not found in cases of renal albuminuria, because a sufficiently careful search has not been made. In suspected cases, several slides should be thoroughly examined before a positive conclusion is drawn. A magnifying power of at least one sixth objective should be used in the examination for casts ; it saves time, however, to first look over the slide with a lower power, and then to examine more closely with a higher power all suspected objects.

Various accidental constituents, as fibres of cotton, linen, and wool, and hair, may be mistaken for casts. They are distinguished by their general appearance and the character of their ends, which are generally square or broken and ragged, while those of casts are more or less round, even, and smooth.

65. SPERMATOZOA.—They are about 50 μ in length (7 times the diameter of a red blood-cell), and consist of a pear-shaped head and a long tapering tail. They may be found in the urine after coitus and emissions, and in the vaginal secretion after connection.

66. FRAGMENTS OF TUMORS.—They are very rarely seen in the urine, and are of no practical clinical value on account of the difficulty involved in their recognition.

67. MICRO-ORGANISMS (fermentative and pathogenic fungi).—Healthy urine when voided is free from fungi, but after a time it contains many fermentative fungi, of which the micrococcus ureæ and bacterium ureæ are most active in transforming urea into carbonate of am-

monia. Specific pathogenic fungi have also been detected in the urine in erysipelas, relapsing fever, typhoid, and tuberculosis (*vide* Part VI.).

68. CHEMICAL EXAMINATION.—A determination of the principal constituents of the urine can be quickly made by reactions carried out in a test-tube, or with a small amount in a watch-glass, water being added if necessary.

Fill a Test-Tube Half-Full of Turbid Urine, and Heat.	Appearance of Deposit.	Confirmatory Tests Applied to the Deposit.	Reaction of Urine.
I.—The turbidity disappears— Urates.	Brick-red deposit.	Murexide test.	Usually acid.
II.—The turbidity remains. A few drops of conc. acetic acid are added ;			
a. The turbidity disappears— Earthy phosphates.	White deposit.	Dissolves without effervescence.	Neutral or alkaline.
" carbonates.	White deposit.	Dissolves with effervescence.	Alkaline.
Urate of ammonia (slowly soluble).	—	Soluble in hydrochloric-acid and murexide test.	Alkaline.
b. The turbidity remains— Uric acid.	Cayenne pepper.	Murexide test.	Acid.
Oxalate of lime.	White deposit.	Dissolves in hydrochloric acid.	Acid.
Organized sediment— Mucus.	Flocculent deposit.	The sediment partly or wholly dissolves on the addition of caustic potash.	Usually alkaline.
Pus.	White deposit.	A stringy gelatinous mass forms on the addition of caustic potash.	Generally alkaline.
Blood.	Red deposit.	See blood in urine.	Acid or alkaline.
Albumin.	—	Various tests.	Acid or alkaline.

69. MICRO-CHEMICAL EXAMINATION.—Most of the crystals are recognized by the microscopical examination after careful study of their shapes. The micro-

chemical examination is however of value in doubtful cases. Place a drop of the reagent at the edge of the cover glass and observe the changes resulting from its gradual penetration beneath the cover glass. A piece of filtering paper placed at the opposite side of the cover glass hastens the action.

1. A drop of strong acetic acid dissolves :
   a. Of the crystalline
      constituents .... Triple phosphates.
      Ammonium urates (slowly with precipitation of uric acid afterwards).
   b. Of the amorphous
      constituents .... Earthy phosphates.
      " carbonates (with effervescence).
      Urates (with precipitation of uric acid afterwards).

2. A drop of hydrochloric acid to a new preparation of the same specimen dissolves in addition to the above —calcium oxalate.

3. Not dissolved by acetic acid and hydrochloric acid.

   Uric acid, the majority of the uncommon sediment and the organized sediment.

VI.—Urinary Calculi.

70. Division according to their chemical formation :
1. Cystin stones—smooth, faintly yellow, not very hard ; seldom occur.

2. Oxalate stones—composed of calcium oxalate ; the smaller are smooth and light brown (hemp-seed stone) ; the larger are rough and jagged, very hard and often dark brown from the coloring matter of the blood (the mulberry stone). They constitute about 3 per cent. of all the stones.

3. Urate stones—consist of uric acid alone or combined with urates. Hard, generally smooth, and of a yellow to reddish-brown color. Stones which are composed only of ammonium urate (in children) are small, soft, and of a light yellow color. They comprise about three fifths of all the calculi.

4. Phosphatic stones—composed of earthy phosphates and triple phosphates. They are rough like sand, grayish-white, and separate easily in layers. Pure phosphatic stones are very rare.

5. Mixed stones.—They consist of strata of different formation, generally of a nucleus of uric acid or calcium oxalate (primary stone formation) and a peripheral layer of earthy and triple phosphates (the secondary stone formation). They form about two fifths of all the stones.

71. EXAMINATION OF CALCULI.—The calculus is triturated to a powder. Large stones are divided by sawing, and separate examinations made of the nuclear and the cortical substance.

1. Heat some of the powder on a platinum foil to red heat.

    a. It ignites and leaves a slight or no sediment.

        Uric acid.

        Cystin (burns with a blue-green flame and has a sharp prussic acid odor).

        Ammonium urates.

        Other urates (leave behind a sediment).

    b. It does not ignite or only incompletely (becomes black), and leaves a considerable sediment insoluble in water.

        Calcium oxalate (sediment effervesces when treated with an acid).

        Earthly phosphates.

        Triple   "

2. Another part of the powder is gently heated with diluted hydrochloric acid for some time and allowed to cool, to precipitate any of the dissolved uric acid.

    a. Remains undissolved.

        Uric acid (try murexide test).

    b. Dissolved..........Cystin.

        Calcium carbonate (with effervescence of gas).

        Calcium oxalate.

        Earthly phosphates.

        Triple   "

        Traces of uric acid.

To distinguish the above substances, the solution should be diluted, super-saturated with ammonia, then slightly acidulated with acetic acid.

Remain dissolved.......Earthy phosphates.

        Triple   "

Distinguish after standing
    some time...........Calcium oxalate (amor-
              phous or crystalline in-
              soluble in ammonia).
            Cystin (six-sided plates
              soluble in ammonia).
            Iron phosphates (flaky
              precipitate, generally
              only present when hy-
              drochloric acid contain-
              ing iron is used).

72. DIAGNOSTIC TABLE OF DIFFUSE DISEASES OF THE KIDNEYS. *

Condition of the Urine.	Hyperæmia.	Acute Nephritis.	Chronic Nephritis.			Amyloid Degeneration of the Kidney.
			Chronic Nephritis—large white kidney.	Secondary contracted kidney.	Primary Contracted Kidney, developing slowly from the beginning.	
Ætiology.	Diseases of the heart and lungs; thrombosis of renal vein or inferior vena cav.	Severe cold; acute poisoning (cantharides, etc.); acute infection (scarlet fever, pneumonia, typhoid, diphtheria, sepsis, etc.)	Acute nephritis (scarlet fever, etc.) continuous exposure (damp dwellings, etc.) intermittent fever, valvular disease, phthisis.		Gout. Saturnismus. Alcoholism. Pyelitis (Lithiasis). Syphilis.	Suppuration as caries; pulmonary phthisis syphilis, (especially amyloid contracted kidney), rarely malaria, carcinoma, abscess, etc.
Quantity.	Much diminished.	Much diminished.	A little less than normal, about 32 oz.	Increased, or at least normal.	Much increased.	Usually about normal. Variable.
Color.	Dark red.	Pale red to dark red, turbid.	Pale red, cloudy.	Pale and transparent.	Pale and transparent.	Light yellow, transparent.
Spec. gravity	High.	High.	A little higher than normal, or normal.	A little less than normal.	Low.	Normal or less.
Blood.	Absent, there may be a few red blood cells	Abundant,	Usually considerable.	Usually little blood.	Red blood cells generally absent.	Absent.
Albumin.	In moderate but variable quantity.	Large quantity.	Considerable.	Moderate quantity.	A very small quantity.	At times absent, but usually considerable
Deposit (Casts, etc.)	Moderate — hyaline casts. A few red blood cells; urates.	Abundant — blood casts, epithelial casts (pure or degenerated). Many red and white blood cells; urates.	Abundant — casts of all kinds, many degenerated. White and red blood cells.	Moderately abundant. Many casts of all kinds.	Very little—hyaline casts especially.	Generally entirely wanting. A few hyaline and fat casts, leucocytes.
Solids.	About normal. Urea increased relatively but not absolutely.	Marked decrease in the amount of urea, chlorides and phosphates.	Diminished in quantity.	Marked diminution in quantity.	Marked diminution in quantity.	Normal, except when formation of urates, etc., is decreased by the poor general condition.

* Leube's Specielle Diagnose.

73

DIAGNOSTIC TABLE OF DIFFUSE DISEASES OF THE KIDNEYS—*Continued.*

Hypertrophy of the heart.	Depends upon the primary disease.	Absent, almost without exception.	Occasionally present.	Usually present.	Present almost without exception.	Absent, except in amyloid contracted kidney.
Hydrops.	Depends upon the primary disease; more stationary, especially in lower extremities.	Marked, rarely entirely absent; location variable.	Marked; ascites.	Moderate, as anasarca and ascites.	Usually absent. It may appear later, due to cardiac insufficiency.	Usually marked.
Uræmia.	Absent.	Common, especially after scarlet fever and colds.	Moderately frequent.	Frequent.	Very frequent.	Absent, except in amyloid contracted kidney.
Additional Symptoms.	General hyperæmia (hyperæmia of the liver, etc.)	Symptoms due to the infectious disease or to the irritant poison.	Marked pallor of the skin, retinitis, bronchitis, etc., inflammation of internal organs.			Retinitis absent. Symptoms of the primary disease (see ætiology).
Death results from.	Cardiac weakness, infarct, etc.	Uræmia, inflammation of internal organs, œdema of the lungs, pneumonia.	Uræmia, or more often inflammation of internal organs.	Uræmia, cerebral hemorrhage, cardiac insufficiency, inflammation of internal organs.		Primary disease, exhaustion.

* This table is of value in that it permits the grouping together of the diseases of the kidneys, and shows at a glance their general differential symptomatology. Diseased processes, however, do not allow any table to be an infallible guide in every case,

Part II.—STOMACH CONTENTS.

1. After the ingestion of a meal containing albuminoids and carbohydrates (fats are not affected by the gastric digestion), amyloid digestion occurs, due to the ptyalin of the saliva, and the starches are gradually converted into dextrine and grape sugar. This period lasts on the average three quarters of an hour, varying, however, with the size of the meal. The fermentation of the grape sugar with the formation of lactic acid due to micro-organisms also ensues.

The gastric mucous membrane begins to secrete hydrochloric acid and pepsin, which is active only in an acid medium, as soon as food enters the stomach. The hydrochloric acid is at first combined, but after one half to three quarters of an hour free hydrochloric acid is present in appreciable quantity. The diastatic power of the saliva and the fermentative action of the micro-organisms cannot proceed in an acid medium. The lactic acid disappears in an hour, and after this time is not present or only traces of it are found. The quantity of free hydrochloric acid continues to increase and reaches its maximum, .15 to .25 per cent., two to three hours after the ingestion of a meal.

2. EXAMINATION OF THE STOMACH.—For a complete examination of the stomach it is necessary to determine :

    a THE MUSCULAR POWER OF THE STOMACH.

    b THE ABSORBENT POWER OF THE STOMACH.

    c THE POWER OF SECRETION AND DIGESTION.

3. To estimate the muscular power of the stomach the Leube test-meal of 10 ounces of soup, 5 ounces of beefsteak, 1⅔ ounces of bread, and 5 ounces of water may be given. After 6 to 7 hours the stomach should be washed out. If the stomach is normal, none or only traces of the food should be found. This test is also used to determine the power of absorption of the stomach.

Riegel employs this test-meal to estimate the gastric power of secretion and digestion. In such cases he washes out the stomach at the height of digestion four to five hours after the ingestion of the meal. The Ewald test-breakfast, however, on account of its simplicity and unvarying character, is much more commonly employed for this purpose. It consists of 9 drachms of bread and 10 ounces of warm water or very weak tea. The stomach contents should be removed in an hour and examined.

4. The removal of the stomach contents is probably best accomplished by " Ewald's method of expression." This consists of pressure upon the abdomen and active expression by the patient, and usually suffices to push the contents of the stomach into the tube. A long soft rubber tube of large calibre having several openings is usually employed. The fenestræ at the end of the tube and in the side close to the end should be smoothly rounded so as not to irritate the mucous membrane. The tube is dipped in warm water and gently passed into the mouth as far back as possible and held there for a second or two. Then when the patient begins to swallow it can be rapidly and easily passed with gentle pressure into the stomach. If the stomach is well filled, the contents will rise in the tube immediately upon its introduction. If the stomach is only partially filled, moderate pressure over the abdomen is usually sufficient to bring up the gastric contents through the tube. If this procedure is not successful, the stomach should be washed out with a small but known quantity of lukewarm water. To accomplish this, fill the tube and funnel, held up high, with water, and before the funnel is entirely empty reverse it into a receptacle on the floor and by syphonic action obtain the gastric contents. If sufficient power is

not secured, it can be increased by inverting the funnel in a vessel containing water, pushing the tube farther into the stomach, and raising the funnel in the water.

Einhorn has devised an ingenious method for obtaining a small quantity of the stomach contents. He employs a small silver receptacle called a stomach bucket (Fig. 22), which is swallowed by the patient an hour after taking the Ewald test-breakfast. The bucket is attached to a cord by which it is drawn up after having been sufficiently long in the stomach.

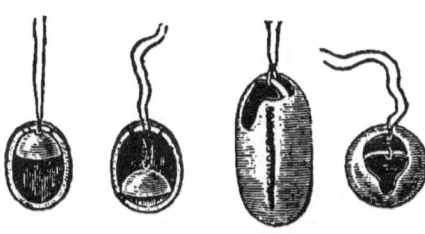

FIG. 22.—EINHORN'S STOMACH BUCKET.

The author thus describes the procedure. The patient is asked to open his mouth widely and the little vessel is placed on the root of the tongue (almost in the pharynx); the patient is now to swallow once. The vessel comes after a short time (one half to one and one half minutes) into the stomach. This point can be easily determined by the length of the thread from the vessel to the mouth as a knot is made on the cord marking 40 ctm., the usual distance from the teeth to the cardia. When this knot is within the mouth, the vessel is certainly in the stomach. It is then left for about five minutes in the stomach and thereupon withdrawn. During the withdrawal of the vessel a resistance is usually felt at the introitus œsophagi. This resistance is overcome if the patient either deeply expires or swallows once when the vessel reaches this constriction. By the act of swallowing the larynx is pushed forward and upward and thus the passage becomes free. The quantity of gastric contents thus obtained is generally sufficient to determine the presence of free hydrochloric acid. This method is especially recommended in nervous patients and in cases of suspected gastric ulcer.

5. The absorbent power of the gastric mucous membrane is determined by the iodide of potassium test of Penzoldt. Iodide of potassium is prescribed in gelatine

capsules and the saliva is tested every five minutes for a trace of the drug. This test is easily made with filtering paper saturated with a starch solution. The prepared paper is moistened with saliva and touched with fuming nitric acid. Normally the first reaction, blue coloration of the filtering paper, appears in 6 to 11½ minutes if the stomach is empty, or in 20 to 45 minutes if the stomach is full. Iodide of potassium in keratin-coated pills may be used to estimate the muscular power of the stomach. The coating is not soluble in the gastric juice and therefore the iodide of potassium is not absorbed until it reaches the small intestine. It has been found, however, that these pills are sometimes dissolved in the stomach.

Ewald advises the administration of salol to determine the muscular sufficiency of the stomach. This is a phenol-salicylate which is not affected by acid fluids but is split up by the pancreatic secretion into salicylic acid and phenol. Therefore, if phenol and salicyluric acid appear in the urine, the salol must have passed from the stomach into the intestine and there been absorbed.

Under normal conditions salicyluric acid appears in the urine 40–75 minutes after the ingestion of 15 grains of salol, which is best given in capsules during digestion. This method has been found inexact, as the intestinal contents must be alkaline to act upon salol, and this is influenced by the intensity of the reaction and the quantity of chyme as well as by the quantity of bile and pancreatic secretion.

Huber has, however, found that salicyluric acid after the ingestion of salol continues in the urine for 24 hours in healthy persons, while in patients with weakened gastric muscular power it may continue for 48 hours or even longer.

It is recommended to examine the urine 30 hours after the administration of salol. If the result is positive an affection of the muscular power of the stomach is in all probability present. If the result is negative the total urine excreted between the 30th and 40th hours must be examined.

6. To estimate the gastric power of secretion and

digestion it is necessary to subject the gastric juice to chemical examination, in order to determine the state of the normal constituents and the presence of abnormal elements.

1. DETERMINATION OF HYDROCHLORIC ACID.—Litmus paper is not suitable for this purpose, as it indicates the presence also of facid salts and organic acids.

A number of dyes, however, do not react with acid salts, and are affected by organic acids only when these acids are in much greater concentration than the mineral acids.

The organic acids (lactic, acetic, butyric acids) react only when there is more than .5 per cent. of the acid present. This never occurs in the gastric contents, as the fermentation which produces these acids is stopped when .5 per cent. of these acids is present. Hydrochloric acid, however, reacts when present in a few hundreds of 1 per cent., providing that it is in a free state and not combined even with such weak organic bases as albumin or peptone.

The following reagents, of which phloroglucin-vanilla is the best, determine the presence only of the free acids. Small quantities of organic acids may be overlooked, as their importance, compared with that of the hydrochloric acid, is small. Larger quantities should be first removed by repeated shaking with ether (5–7 ounces).

a *Methyl-Aniline-Violet Test.*—The violet color of an aqueous solution of methyl-aniline is changed to a blue if .03 per cent. hydrochloric acid is present, to a green if there is .5 per cent. present, and decolorized by 1 per cent. Organic acids affect the color of this solution only when present in large quantities, *i.e.*, if .5 per cent. of lactic acid or 2.5 per cent. of acetic acid is present.

PROCEDURE.—Add to 5–10 c.c. ($1\frac{1}{4}$–$2\frac{1}{2}$ drachms) of water 2–3 drops of a concentrated aqueous solution of methyl-violet. The water assumes a distinctly violet color. Mix equal quantities of the methyl-violet solution and the filtered contents of the stomach. If the mixture becomes decidedly blue, the presence of more than .03 per cent. of hydrochloric acid is proven. The change in color is easily recognized by a comparison of the two solutions.

b *Congo-Paper Test.*—Congo-red is changed to blue by free acids but not by acid salts. .05 per cent. of hydrochloric acid changes congo-red to a dark-blue, smaller quantities produce a faintly blue or violet color.

Organic acids, in quantities less than .5 per cent. have no effect, or (lactic acid) produce only a violet color, which can be removed by washing ; if in greater concentration, which never occurs in the stomach, they produce a dark-blue. This test is made easily with paper which has been colored with congo-red after the manner of reagent paper.

Procedure.—Allow a drop of the gastric secretion to fall on the congo paper. It is colored an intensely dark-blue (*i.e.*, a dark-blue spot appears) if hydrochloric acid, at least .05 per cent., is present. If there is only a faintly blue spot, or if only the border of the spot is dark-blue (a blue ring), a free acid is present. Whether the acid present is hydrochloric acid or an organic acid or a mixture of both cannot be determined by this test.

c *Tropæolin-Paper Test.*—A yellow to reddish-yellow aqueous solution of tropæolin (oo) is changed on the addition of .02 per cent. of hydrochloric acid to a rose- or brownish-red. Organic acids, in less quantity than .5 per cent., exhibit a yellow coloration. The test is readily made with strips of paper placed a short time before use in an alcoholic solution of this dye and then dried. Prolonged saturation weakens their sensitiveness. A good preparation of the dye should be used.

PROCEDURE.—If the spot affected is colored immediately a dark brownish-red, and after drying in a watch-glass over a small flame a lilac color, the presence of at least .05 per cent. hydrochloric acid is shown. Organic acids, only when highly concentrated, produce a faintly brown coloration, but not the lilac coloration when heated.

d *Phloro-Glucin Vanilla* (*Gunzburg's*) *Test.*—A few drops of the reagent, consisting of 2 parts of phloro-glucin and 1 part of vanilla in 30 parts (by weight) of alcohol, and an equal quantity of filtered gastric secretion are carefully evaporated in a porcelain dish over a flame ; .01 per cent. of hydrochloric acid produces a beautiful red tinge. Organic acids, even when present in large quantity, do not give a reaction.

On heating any albuminous solution strongly, a deep-red, central coloration appears after evaporation. This should not be confounded with the hydrochloric-acid reaction, which has the appearance of red streaks or a corresponding red blush at the edges on gently heating or slowly evaporating to dryness.

This reaction permits an approximate quantitative estimate of the amount of free acid. By successive dilutions of the contents of the stomach giving Gunzburg's reaction to $\frac{1}{3}$, $\frac{1}{5}$, $\frac{1}{10}$, etc., until the reaction is no longer perceptible, the quantity of free hydrochloric acid can be approximately estimated as the limit of the reaction is about .05 per mille. If the red coloration is still obtained with the one twentieth solution, the gastric juice contains 1.0 per mille or 0.1 per cent. of free hydrochloric acid. A rough guess at the quantity of the acid can be made by the intensity of the color.

e *Resorcin Test.*—Boäs recommends a solution of resorcin 5, white sugar 3, and diluted alcohol to 100. Three to five drops of this solution are added to five or six drops of the contents of the stomach, and treated in the same way as in the preceding test. If 0.05 per mille

6

of free hydrochloric acid is present, a rose coloration appears. This is never produced by organic acids, however concentrated.

2. LACTIC ACID.—a *Iron Chloride Test.*—One drop of liquor ferri sesquichloridi gives to 50 c.c. (1⅜ ounces) of water a faintly yellow tinge. If equal parts of this solution and one containing .01 per cent. lactic acid are mixed, the mixture has a decidedly yellow color. Acetic acid, butyric acid, and acid salts, in concentration up to .3 per cent., do not change the color. Albuminous bodies, salts, peptones, and the like, have but little effect upon this reaction. This test is valuable for the detection of lactic acid in the gastric contents.

b *Iron-Chloride and Carbolic-Acid Test.*—A solution consisting of one drop of liquor ferri sesquichloridi, 2½ drachms of a 4-per-cent. solution of carbolic acid (or 4 drops of acid. carbolic. liq.), and 5 drachms of water has an amethyst blue color when freshly prepared.

If equal parts of this solution and of filtered gastric secretion containing .01 per cent. lactic acid are mixed, the mixture assumes a yellow or greenish-yellow color. The other acids which are present in the gastric secretion (hydrochloric, acetic, butyric acids) produce only a light yellow or a grayish-yellow color even if .3 per cent. is present. The carbolic acid reaction (blue color) must disappear before the characteristic reaction (yellow color) of the lactic acid can be observed.

3. ACETIC AND BUTYRIC ACIDS.—A not too small quantity of the filtered gastric juice is shaken with a large quantity of ether. If organic acids are present, a fluid residue having an acid reaction remains after evaporation. This has a characteristic odor, if volatile butyric acid is present. Its presence can be determined by special reactions.

a ACETIC ACID.—Dissolve a portion of the residue in water, neutralize exactly, and add a drop of iron perchloride. If acetic acid is present, it becomes blood-red, and on boiling a brownish-red precipitate of basic ferric acetate appears.

Formic acid produces the same color. But the diagnostic importance of this reaction is not thereby affected, for if this acid is found in the stomach contents—which up to this time has not been the case—its presence, like that of acetic and butyric acid, can be due only to an acid fermentation in the stomach.

b BUTYRIC ACID.—Dissolve the remainder of the residue in one or two drops of water and add a small piece of calcium chloride. The butyric acid separates from the rest and swims on the surface as small globules of oil on account of its insolubility in salt solutions.

4. DETERMINATION OF THE TOTAL ACIDITY.—This is practically a quantitative test of the hydrochloric acid if it is present in any amount, as other acids present can usually be disregarded. To 5–10 c.c. (1–25 drachms) of filtered gastric contents a one tenth normal solution of caustic soda is added from a burette until neutralized. This point is easily determined if a drop of an alcoholic solution of phenolphthalein has been previously added. the solution remains colorless while acid or neutral, but becomes red when alkaline. Normally 4–6.5 c.c. of this alkaline solution is required for 10 c.c. of gastric contents (each c.c. = .00365 grm. HCl).

5. DIGESTIVE POWER.—Free hydrochloric acid and pepsin are necessary for peptonizing albumin. Experience has shown that an inability of the gastric juice to digest is due to a defect in the acid, as a complete absence of pepsin has very rarely been observed. The digestive test is therefore only another test for hydrochloric acid. It permits by the rapidity of its action a more reliable estimate of its quantity than the intensity of the color reaction allows. The result obtained from the determination of hydrochloric acid by the color reaction and that deduced from the test of the digestive power will practically always agree with one exception, *i. e.*, where lactic acid, which is completely free (not combined with albumin) is present. This acid in contradistinction to the other organic acids acts with pepsin almost as vigorously as hydrochloric acid. A gastric secretion which contains pepsin and lactic acid, but no

hydrochloric acid, can still digest very well, but is abnormal in spite of that fact.

a *Carmine Fibrin Test.*—Fibrin, which has been obtained in flakes by whipping blood, is washed with water until colorless, and then placed in an ammoniacal solution of carmine for twenty-four hours. After removal from this solution the fibrin is repeatedly washed with water until it ceases to color the water. The flakes, still a dark red, are placed in glycerine where they can be preserved unchanged for years. They should be thoroughly washed with water before their use. The coloring material has so completely permeated the fibrin that it cannot be removed by any solvent, not even by diluted hydrochloric acid. It is only after the fibrin has been digested that the solution containing it becomes colored, and the digestive power of the fluid thus becomes apparent. The carmine fibrin is a very delicate reagent for the determination of the digestive power.

PROCEDURE.—Wash thoroughly with water some of the flakes of carmine fibrin, and place them in a .2 per cent. solution of hydrochloric acid. Remove the excess of acid by pressing with the fingers, and place the fibrin in a test-tube. Put a like quantity of fibrin, thoroughly washed with water but not treated with hydrochloric acid, in another test-tube. Pour into both of the test-tubes 5–10 c.c. ($1\frac{1}{4}$–$2\frac{1}{2}$ drachms) of the filtered gastric contents. If the gastric secretion contains hydrochloric acid and pepsin in sufficient quantity, the fibrin will be partially dissolved, giving a red coloration to the fluid within five minutes at the temperature of the room. If the digestion is active, all the fibrin is quickly dissolved. If the red coloration appears only in the test-tube containing the fibrin treated with hydrochloric acid, the gastric juice is deficient in hydrochloric acid; if the reaction also fails in this test-tube, the gastric juice is deficient both in pepsin and hydrochloric acid.

b. *Egg-Albumin Test.*—The albumin of boiled eggs is divided into small disks $\frac{2}{3}$ of an inch in diameter and $\frac{1}{25}$ of an inch thick. These can be preserved in glycerine in the same manner as the fibrin. They are much less soluble than the fibrin flakes in the gastric juice, and require for their solution, if the gastric juice is active, $\frac{1}{2}$–1 hour at 100° F. An exact differentiation in the digestive power can therefore easily be made by this test.

PROCEDURE.—Wash thoroughly the disks of albumin with water, and place two of them in each of two test-tubes, add 10 c.c. (2$\frac{1}{2}$ drachms) of filtered gastric secretion to both. 1–2 drops of concentrated (25 per cent.) hydrochloric acid are added to the contents of one of the test-tubes. They are then placed in a thermostat heated to 100° F. If pepsin is present in sufficient quantity, the disks should be dissolved, after 1–2 hours, at least in the test-tube to which the hydrochloric acid has been added.

6. RENNET FERMENT.—Add a few drops of the filtered gastric juice to some fresh milk (3–4 drachms); if the rennet ferment is present, curdling will occur in a few minutes.

7. BILE.—(a) Bile pigment is detected by Gmelin's test. If the reaction of the gastric contents is acid the larger part remains insoluble in the sediment. It should therefore first be dissolved by the addition of diluted alkalies, and then the test be applied. The bile pigment does not usually appear in the form of bilirubin but· in that of biliverdin, as is evident by the green color. The color reaction accordingly begins with a blue ring. The bile pigment can be extracted from the solid gastric contents by warm alcohol with the addition of some drops of diluted sulphuric acid. The extract is a beautiful green to bluish-green solution of biliverdin.

(b) Biliary acids are detected by Pettenkofer's reaction. Evaporate some of the fluid in a small porcelain dish, after the addition of 1–3 drops of diluted sulphuric acid (16 per cent.) and of a very small quantity of cane-sugar, with continuous shaking over a small flame at a temperature of 60°–80° C. (140°–176° F.). If biliary acids are present, in amount over .05 per cent., a beautiful purplish-red color appears immediately or during the evaporation at about the point of dryness. Overheating must be avoided by continuous shaking, also the addition of too much sugar, as in either case a black product may result, which disguises this reaction.

Albuminous bodies, peptone, and many other organic compounds give a similar color. If they are present, the Pettenkofer's test is not reliable, and the biliary acids must first be isolated.

8. HÆMOGLOBIN (BLOOD).—Unaltered hæmoglobin is found in the gastric contents only in vomitus following quickly large hemorrhages. It is changed in most cases to a product resembling coffee-grounds, the color of which is due to the formation of hæmatin.

(1) Determination by the test for hæmin.

A drop of the sediment is dried on a slide by gentle heat, the further procedure is the same as 16, 4.

(2) Determination by Heller's Test (*vide* page 21).

Make an extract of the sediment with diluted caustic soda. If hæmatin is present, the extract has a brown color. Filter, add an equal volume of normal urine (in order to supply earthy phosphates), and boil. If hæmatin is present, the phosphates are precipitated in beautiful red crystals.

9. AMMONIUM CARBONATE.—This is present in the stomach in cases of uræmia and cholera as a result of the metamorphosis of urea. The addition of caustic soda to the stomach contents volatilizes the ammonia, which is recognized by its penetrating odor and by the formation of a haze on a glass rod moistened with acetic or hydrochloric acid. This haze is due to the union and condensation of the gaseous ammonia and the vapor either of the acetic or hydrochloric acid forming either the acetate or the chlorate of ammonium.

Traces of ammonia may be detected in the following manner : a piece of red litmus paper is stuck on the convex side of a watch-glass. This is placed on a wide test-tube which contains some of the gastric contents, to which a few drops of caustic soda have been added. The ammonia is evolved on the addition of the caustic soda, and changes the color of the test paper.

It should always be remembered that no matter how complete our chemical apparatus or how scientific our procedure, we cannot duplicate in test-tubes the conditions existing in the human organism. The results obtained in artificial digestion must always be imperfect, and our deductions should therefore be correspondingly conservative.

7. Vierordt gives the following as of diagnostic value :

1. When examination shows that the duration of digestion is not lengthened, digestion is generally normal. It may, however, be shortened, and this condition occurs at times with hyperacidity.

2. When free hydrochloric acid is absent at the normally highest point of digestion, it may be due to :

(a) Complete destruction of the gastric mucous membrane, as in atrophy and in amyloid degeneration of the stomach (constant).

(b) Carcinoma of the stomach with dilatation (almost constant), other forms of dilatation (very often), and of these especially chronic catarrh.

3. Diminished acidity (even absence) has been observed in :

(a) Severe forms of anæmia
(b) Fever
(c) Certain cases of nervous dyspepsia.

4. Hyperacidity has been noticed in :

(a) Most of the cases of gastric ulcer
(b) Certain forms of nervous dyspepsia
(c) Acute and at times chronic gastric catarrh.

Thanks to the new method of examination by means of the stomach-tube, the knowledge of diseases of the stomach has been greatly advanced and the differentiation of their pathological conditions made much more reliable. It is nevertheless natural that much is still the subject of controversy in a field which has been investigated in a scientific manner only in the last decade.   There is also the danger that symptoms found in individual cases will be considered diagnostic of the disease.   Thus it is with the alleged increased acid secretion in ulcer of the stomach and absence of hydrochloric acid in cancer of the stomach.   We should therefore keep in mind that this or that hypothesis, which to-day is considered true or very probable, may in course of time prove to be erroneous or require to be essentially modified—" Leube's Specielle Diagnose."

Part III.—FÆCES.

The physical properties and the microscopic examination of the fæces give valuable diagnostic indications, but the chemical examination on account of its complexity is of less value.

1 BILE-PIGMENT.—The bile-pigments, unaltered, are not normally present in the fæces but appear in the form of hydrobilirubin (urobilin), which is not detected by Gmelin's test. They are, however, present in catarrhal conditions of the small intestine and produce the green color of the fæces. As they are soluble in alkalies and insoluble in acids, they are either in the fluid or in the solid part according to the reaction, and may be detected by Gmelin's reaction.

2. ALBUMIN.—Dilute the fæces with a very weak solution of acetic acid, filter repeatedly, and examine the filtrate for albumin.

3. BLOOD.—Blood, coming from the stomach or upper part of the intestines, is in the form of methæmoglobin and hæmatin, and gives a brownish-red to brownish-black color to the fæces. Pure blood occurs only after profuse hemorrhages arising close to the anus.

Its presence is determined as in Part II., 8.

(a) By the hæmin test.

(b) By Heller's test.

4. CRYSTALS.—1. TRIPLE PHOSPHATE. — Occur normally and in different pathological conditions.

For microscopical appearance and chemical character see Part I, 49.

2.—PHOSPHATE OF LIME.—Similar to the above (*vide* Part I, 46).

These and other lime salts are often colored intensely yellow by the bile-pigment.

3. OXALATE OF LIME.—(Envelope shape) due to vegetable food (*vide* Part I, 45).

4. LACTATE OF LIME—Present in enteritis, especially in that of children in the shape of sheaves of fine needles.

5. ORGANIC SALTS OF LIME AND MAGNESIA.—Needles grouped together in tufts and balls, present in large numbers in acholia (pernicious jaundice).

6. CHOLESTERIN.—Crystals, soluble in ether. Recognised easily by means of sulphuric acid and iodine (*vide infra*, 5, I).

7. HÆMATOIDIN—Yellowish-red crystals ; present after intestinal hemorrhage.

8. CHARCOT-LEYDEN CRYSTALS.—The union of a phosphate with an organic base of the formula C_2H_5H. Colorless, faintly brilliant, of pyramidal shape often with convex surface (resembling the small waxy bodies often found in prostatic secretion). Insoluble in cold water, alcohol, ether, or chloroform. Very soluble in acids, alkalies, and in alkaline carbonates.

They occur in pathological conditions ; anæmia, caused by anchylostoma duodenalis, dysentery, typhoid fever, etc. They have also been found in the expectoration especially in bronchial asthma ; in the blood, the spleen, and marrow in leukæmia ; in the excretion of the prostate gland.

A mixture of one drop of this and one drop of a 1-per-cent. solution of ammonium phosphate shows, when examined under the microscope, beautifully shaped crystals immediately or after an hour. Their detection is of value in differentiating prostatarrhœa from gonorrhœa.

5. CONCRETIONS.—Dilute the fæces with water to the consistency of a thin pulp and strain through muslin to find stones.

1. GALL-STONES.—They consist principally of calcium carbonate combined in varying quantities with cholesterin and bilirubin ; the nucleus contains a larger proportion of lime combined with bilirubin. They are of a whitish-yellow, seldom of a brownish-red color, greasy to the touch, with glistening lines of fracture, and weigh proportionately much less than other stones. If a portion is heated on a platinum foil, it melts and ignites with a flame leaving an ash.

For a complete chemical analysis, they are broken up and boiled in water. to dissolve traces of biliary acids and other matter. The sediment is treated with a mixture of equal volumes of ether and alcohol. The cholesterin is dissolved, the biliary coloring matter (principally bilirubin) combined with calcium remains undissolved.

The cholesterin is crystallized usually in large, thin, rhomboidal plates, less often into glistening needles when the solution is diluted. Place some of the cholesterin on a slide, and add concentrated (80 %) sulphuric acid, the edges of the plates dissolve, and the plates become carmine red, which is changed to violet on the addition of Lugol's solution.

The bilirubin-calcium is dissolved in diluted hydrochloric acid, and the bilirubin removed by chloroform. It can then be crystallized or subjected to Gmelin's test.

2. INTESTINAL STONES. They consist usually of an organic nucleus (fruit stone, blood coagulum, hardened

fæcal mass) and peripheral layers of earthy and triple phosphates. To determine its composition, the stone should be divided. One portion should be subjected on a platinum foil to heat, and another part to diluted hydrochloric acid at a gentle heat. The phosphates are dissolved, the cholesterin and nuclear substance are insoluble, and must be subjected to a microscopical examination.

Part IV.—THE BLOOD.

1. The blood is an alkaline fluid, whose specific gravity ranges from 1035–1068, and which constitutes about one thirteenth of the body-weight. Its color is either bright red (arterial blood) or dark red (venous blood), depending upon the state of the hæmoglobin. The hæmoglobin is contained in the red blood-cells, and forms a loose combination with the oxygen of the air called oxy-hæmoglobin, which is bright red. As the blood circulates, the hæmoglobin gives up almost all its oxygen to the tissues, and as a result the blood becomes dark red.

Changes in the quantity or quality of the blood are of the greatest clinical importance, as such changes affect the functions of the blood ; the carrying of oxygen from the air to the tissues, the conveying of nutrient material from the alimentary tract to the rest of the body, and the transporting of the products of combustion to the principal excretory organs,—the lungs and the kidneys.

THE ELEMENTS OF THE BLOOD.—The blood consists of a nearly colorless liquid, the plasma, red and white cells (leucocytes), and the so-called blood-plates ; of these, the blood-plasma and blood-plates are as yet of no clinical importance.

2. RED BLOOD-CELLS.—They are bi-concave disks with rounded edge, and of an average diameter of 7–8 μ. They usually arrange themselves on a slide in rows like rolls of coin, and singly look like circular plates if flat, and biscuit-shaped if on edge. When brought within

focus, they have a light centre and dark periphery. The individual cells are pale yellow, of homogeneous structure, and without nuclei. The red blood-cells at the periphery of a preparation become shrunken and crenated due to evaporation, while, upon the addition of water, they swell and lose their central concavity. There are normally in the male about 5,000,000, and in the female 4,500,000 red blood-cells in a cubic millimetre of blood.

Pathological Changes in the Red Blood-Cells.—The number may be increased (policythæmia) or diminished (oligocythæmia), the size

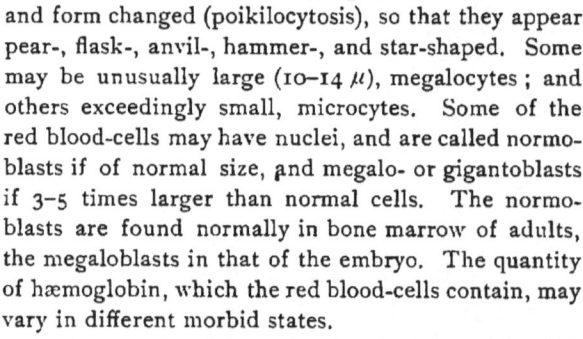

and form changed (poikilocytosis), so that they appear pear-, flask-, anvil-, hammer-, and star-shaped. Some may be unusually large (10–14 μ), megalocytes ; and others exceedingly small, microcytes. Some of the red blood-cells may have nuclei, and are called normoblasts if of normal size, and megalo- or gigantoblasts if 3–5 times larger than normal cells. The normoblasts are found normally in bone marrow of adults, the megaloblasts in that of the embryo. The quantity of hæmoglobin, which the red blood-cells contain, may vary in different morbid states.

An increased number of red cells in a cubic millimetre of blood occurs in conditions of hunger, and in states marked by a depletion of the system of watery elements, as in cholera and dysentery. A diminution in number may be due to a direct loss of blood as after hemorrhage, to a decreased formation or increased destruction of red cells as in conditions of mal-nutrition, in infectious diseases, toxicoses,

FIG. 23.—
THOMA-ZEISS
HÆMACYTO-
METER CAPIL-
LARY TUBE.

neoplasms, etc. A change in the shape and size of red blood-cells, and the appearance of nucleated red cells characterize certain pathological conditions.

When any or all of these changes in red blood-cells are marked, an ordinary microscopic preparation made with care will show that the red blood-cells are less numerous, their color paler, their shape unusual, or their normal proportion to the white blood-cells (550 red blood-cells to one white cell) altered. If the changes are slight, or if exact results are desired, special apparatus must be used to determine the degree of oligocythæmia or oligochromæmia (decrease in hæmoglobin). Of the various instruments devised, the Thoma-Zeiss apparatus for counting blood-cells, and the V. Fleischl's, and the Gowers' instruments for determining the percentage of hæmoglobin give the most satisfactory results.

3. THE THOMA-ZEISS HÆMACYTOMETER, an apparatus for counting blood-cells, consists of a glass capillary tube about 10 cm. long (Fig. 23), which at *b* expands to a bulb, containing a freely movable small glass ball. The tube is graduated, and has figures 0.5 and 1 beneath, and 101 above the bulb. A counting space in a receptacle cemented upon a slide completes the apparatus. The floor of this space is divided into squares ; the depth of each is exactly $\frac{1}{10}$ mm., the sides $\frac{1}{20}$ mm., and the volume of each tiny cube $\frac{1}{4000}$ cubic millimetre (Fig. 24).

PROCEDURE.—Blood, obtained by puncturing the thoroughly clean finger, is drawn up either to the mark 0.5 or 1, then the diluting solution (3% Na Cl) to the mark 101, and the tube well shaken. The blood in the capillary tube is blown out and then the counting space filled with the diluted blood and a cover glass carefully pushed over it from the side so

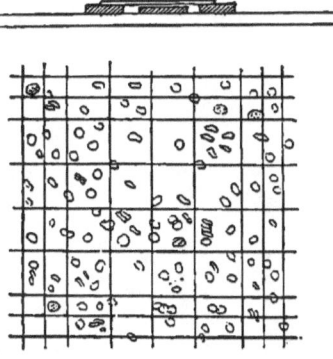

FIG. 24.—THOMA-ZEISS HÆMACYTO-METER. SLIDE FOR COUNTING.

that no air bubbles are included. The preparation is allowed to stand for one or two minutes to permit the red blood-cells to settle and then placed under the microscope. The field is seen to be divided into a number of small squares, arranged in larger squares of 16, marked off by double lines. All the blood cells within a large square of 16 small squares are counted, together with those impinging upon the upper and left borders while those touching the lower and right are disregarded. The greater the number of large squares examined, the more accurate is the result. The common practice is to count the number of cells in 10 large squares (160 small squares). The number of red blood-cells in a cubic millimetre of blood is the result obtained by multiplying the number of red blood-cells counted, by 4000 and by the degree of dilution (100 or 200) and dividing the product by the number of squares taken.

$$X = \frac{N \times 4000 \times 100}{160}$$

X = Number of red blood-cells in a cubic millimetre of blood.

N = Number of red blood-cells in 160 squares.

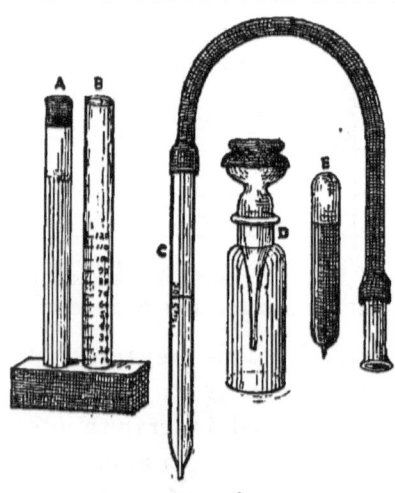

FIG. 25.—GOWERS' HAEMOGLO-BINOMETER.

The white blood-cells can be counted in the same manner and with the same instrument as the red cells, but the liability to error is very much greater as the white blood-cells are so few in number. Several preparations should therefore be made and counted. A capillary tube which allows a dilution of ten-fold has been constructed for counting the white blood-cells. A solution of acetic acid .3 to .5 per cent. to which a small quantity of an aniline dye has been added is employed. This solution dissolves the red blood-cells and stains the white cells. 3–5 preparations should be examined to obtain results of value.

4. GOWERS' HÆMOGLOBINOMETER.—It consists of two glass tubes (Fig. 25, A. and B.) of exactly the same size, one of which contains a carmine-picro-carmine gelatine which has exactly the same tint as a 1-per-cent. aqueous solution of normal blood. The other tube is graduated from 10–120 and receives the blood to be examined and the diluting solution (distilled water). There are in addition a capillary tube (C), a bottle of distilled water with dropper (D), and a needle (E).

PROCEDURE.—The finger is thoroughly cleaned and pricked with the needle and 20 cubic millimetres of blood are drawn into the capillary tube. This is then blown into tube B which should contain a few drops of water. After shaking the tube for a minute, dilute it with distilled water, drop by drop, from the stopper of bottle D, until the tint of the diluted blood is the same as that of the carmine gelatine. If the tints are similar when the tube is filled to the mark 100, the quantity of hæmoglobin is normal ; if it requires greater dilution, the hæmoglobin is in excess, if less dilution, it is below normal in quantity as indicated by the figures of the scale. The tubes should be held before a sheet of white paper when compared and the determination should be made by daylight. The results are only approximate but sufficiently exact for clinical purposes.

5. VON FLEISCHL'S HÆMOMETER.—This apparatus consists of a small stand like that of a microscope with a stage which has a circular opening in the centre, beneath which is a plate of plaster-of-Paris, resembling a mirror, to reflect light. Under the stage is placed a movable wedge of red (Cassius' golden purple) glass in a metallic frame which has a graduated scale. The circular opening in the stage is for a small metallic cylinder with glass bottom, which is divided by a vertical partition into two equal divisions, one of which receives light which has passed through the red glass wedge, while the other receives light directly from the plaster-of-Paris reflector. An automatic capillary tube and a dropper complete the apparatus (Fig. 26).

7

PROCEDURE.—The finger is punctured and the capillary tube filled with blood. The tube, after all the blood on the outside is carefully wiped off, is placed horizontally in one of the divisions of the cylinder, which should contain a little distilled water, and is shaken about to wash out the blood. When most of the blood is removed, hold the tube vertically over the same division and wash it within and without with distilled water from a dropper, thus removing all the blood. Then place the cylinder in

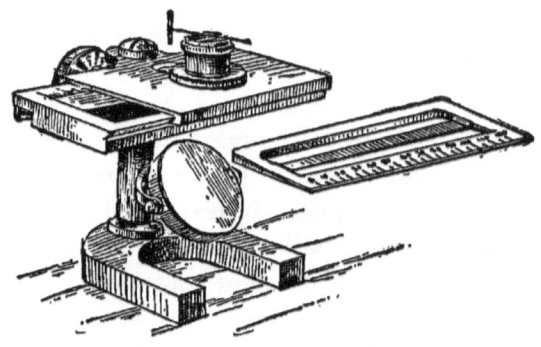

FIG. 26.—VON FLEISCHL'S HÆMOMETER.

the circular opening and fill both divisions to the brim with distilled water. The wedge of red glass is then moved until the tints as they appear through the divisions of the cylinder seem similar. The percentage of hæmoglobin is indicated by the scale. The determination should be made by yellow light (gas or oil).

Care should be taken to always thoroughly wash the capillary tubes with distilled water, alcohol, and ether after use.

6. THE WHITE BLOOD-CELLS (LEUCOCYTES).—They are masses of protoplasm having nuclei and possessing amœboid movements. They vary greatly in size but average about 10 μ in diameter, appear singly in the microscopical field and are recognized by their granular surface. The nuclei are at times seen in fresh preparations and can always be made visible by the addition of diluted acetic acid. Their size and the shape and size of the nuclei divide them into four groups.

A. *Small Lymphocytes.*—Small mononuclear cells about the size of a red blood-cell with a relatively large round nucleus, which is deeply stained by aniline dyes.

B. *Large Lymphocytes.*—Mononuclear cells, about twice the size of the small lymphocytes, with a relatively small oval nucleus. Both this and the preceding group are formed in the lymph glands, the small being regarded as an earlier stage of the large lymphocytes.

C. *Leucocytes with irregular or multiple nuclei.*—They are somewhat larger than the red blood-cells and have strongly refracting, finely granular protoplasm. They have either a single irregular nucleus or several nuclei due to division. This group constitutes the great majority of the white blood-cells.

D. *Leucocytes with coarsely granular protoplasm.*—A small number of group c are characterized by highly refracting, coarsely granular protoplasm. They are called coarsely granular leucocytes or eosinophilic cells.

7. The number of leucocytes in a cubic millimetre of blood ranges normally from 6000 to 10,000, *i. e.*, one to 800–500 red blood-cells. An increase in their number, called leucocytosis, occurs at times in health (*physiological leucocytosis*) and in certain morbid conditions (*pathological leucocytosis*).

Physiological leucocytosis is usually present several hours after the ingestion of food, in the latter part of pregnancy, and in the new-born.

Pathological leucocytosis may be either an accompaniment of diseased processes or the principal symptom of a definite disease (leukæmia).

It is present in chronic cachectic conditions and after repeated hemorrhages.

It may occur in certain inflammatory diseases and is then called *inflammatory leucocytosis.* A marked leucocytosis (15–20,000) is said to characterize inflammations of serous membranes of a suppurative character, a less pronounced leucocytosis those of a sero-fibrinous character, while such inflammations when tubercular show no increase in the number of leucocytes. The most marked inflammatory leucocytosis is found in croupous pneumonia. The increase appears a few hours after the chill and quickly reaches 20,000–30,000 leucocytes in a cubic millimetre of blood. The number decreases markedly in 24 hours but remains until the crisis above normal.[1] Non-exudative inflammatory processes without great inanition, as malaria, measles, and scarlet fever, if uncomplicated, show no increase of leucocytes, while those characterized by pronounced inanition, as typhoid fever, exhibit a marked diminution in leucocytes. Leucocytosis in typhoid fever indicates a complication of a suppurative character. A more or less pronounced leucocytosis has been observed in sepsis, puerperal fever, erysipelas, diphtheria, and recurrent fever.

A very pronounced leucocytosis (35,000–320,000) and a change in the character of the leucocytes are the pathognomonic symptoms of

---

[1] It would seem as if the degree of leucocytosis furnishes us an indication of the effort which the system is able to make in order to overcome the infection. When the degree of leucocytosis in pneumonia is markedly low (under 10,000), the system reveals its inability to react, and the prognosis is therefore almost always fatal. When the degree of leucocytosis is high, it indicates an infection of great severity, but shows the vigorous reaction of the system against the poison, rendering the prognosis favorable unless some complication ensues.

leukæmia. The change in the leucocytes was first shown by Ehrlich, who discovered that the protoplasm of the white cells contain, coarse and fine granules which react differently with aniline dyes, and that similar cells are characterized by the same kind of granules. He therefore classified the leucocytes according to this differential action with aniline stains. Three of these types, which are called after letters of the Greek alphabet, alpha, beta, gamma, etc., are of importance in the investigation of the human blood, and are differentiated from one another by the fact that they are each stained by a pigment of a different reaction and by that alone. They are, therefore also called eosinophile (acid), basophile (basic), or neutrophile (neutral). The knowledge of the increase or appearance of these cells is said to be of great clinical value.

1. THE ALPHA OR EOSINOPHILIC GRANULES.—The protoplasm of these cells is characterized by coarse granules which are stained only by acid aniline dyes, of which eosin is one. They generally have one, at times two, and rarely three nuclei. They are said to have their origin in the marrow and number 2–8 per cent. of the leucocytes in normal blood, but are increased in number in leukæmia.

2. THE GAMMA, MAST CELL, OR BASOPHILIC GRANULES.—Fine granules stained only by basic aniline dyes as dahlia, gentian-violet, etc. They were said to occur only in pathological conditions (leukæmia) in small numbers, but they have also been found, though rarely, in healthy blood.

3. THE EPSILON OR NEUTROPHILIC GRANULES.—They are characterized by very fine granules, one or more very irregular nuclei having the shape of the letters S, V, F, M, etc., and are stained by neutral aniline dyes, *i. e.*, a mixture of acid and basic aniline dyes, as methyl-blue and acid fuchsin. About 70 per cent. of the leucocytes in normal blood belong to this group.

8. EXAMINATION OF BLOOD.—The pulp of the finger or the lobe of the ear should be thoroughly cleaned with alcohol and then punctured with a needle. Cover-glasses, which have been kept in alcohol, are carefully dried, touched to the blood, which should not be pressed out, then inverted on clean slides when preparations of

fresh blood are desired, or immediately covered with other glasses and at once slid apart if permanent preparations are wanted.   Another method consists in passing the edge of one end of a slide through the blood, then in drawing the slide, held at an angle of 45°, quickly across a cover glass, steadied with a finger of the other hand, thus spreading a thin film of blood over the glass.   The film of blood dries very quickly and may be "fixed" for staining either by being placed for 1–2 hours in a mixture of equal parts of alcohol and ether, or being subjected to a temperature of 120° to 130° C. (248° to 266° F.).   This degree of heat is easily obtained by arranging a copper plate (12 x 4 inches) beneath one end of which an alcohol lamp is lit.   In about half an hour the heat of the plate becomes constant, *i. e.*, radiation is equal to conduction, and the boiling point on the plate is where drops of water are immediately converted into steam, beginning, of course, at the end farthest from the flame.   A point an inch nearer the flame than the boiling point will have the desired temperature (about 120° C.).   The glasses are placed, besmeared side uppermost, on this spot and left there for an hour.   They are now ready for staining, and after staining are rinsed in water, dried with filtering paper, and mounted in Canada balsam.

9. STAINING SOLUTIONS.

.1–.5 per cent. aqueous solution of eosin.

The cover-glasses should be floated with besmeared side downward for 10–20 minutes in this solution, then washed in water, dried, and mounted.   If the solution is heated, the time required for staining is shortened.

.2–.5 per cent. alcoholic solution of eosin.

Stains in ½–1 minute.

The red blood-cells are stained a uniform red, the protoplasm of the leucocytes is faintly stained, and the eosinophilic granules a strikingly deep red.

Rieder recommends a method for double staining which gives very satisfactory results. He places a drop or two of a saturated solution of eosin in carbol-glycerine (carbolic acid 5 per cent.) upon a prepared cover-glass and covers it with another besmeared glass. After 24 hours the glasses are separated, washed thoroughly with water and stained for 10–15 minutes in hæmatoxylon (Delafield's) diluted with an equal volume of water. They are then washed, dried, and mounted in Canada balsam. The red blood-cells are stained a uniform eosin red, the eosinophilic granules a strikingly bright red, and the nuclei of the leucocytes a dark purple (Fig. 27, See end of volume.)

The following formulæ are recommended by Ehrlich and other workers in this field.

Czenzynski's solution :

    Methylene blue, concentrated aqueous solution.....40
    ½ per cent. solution of eosin in 70 per cent. alcohol 20
    Distilled water...............................40

This solution gently heated stains in fifteen minutes. The red blood-cells appear eosin-red, the eosinophilic granules bright red, and the nuclei dark blue. A good result is obtained by staining for 2–3 minutes in a heated .5 per cent. alcoholic solution of eosin, and then the same length of time in a saturated aqueous solution of methylene blue.

    Eosin
    Aurantia   } of each................... 2
    Nigrosin (or indulin)
    Glycerine..................................30

This solution acts in 16–24 hours. The red blood-cells are stained orange, the protoplasm of the leucocytes a dirty gray, the nuclei much darker, and the eosinophilic granules a bright red.

Ehrlich's hæmatoxylin-eosin solution :

    Hæmatoxylin... .... 4.–5.
    Glacial acetic acid......................... 20.
    Distilled water
    Alcohol   } of each...................100.
    Glycerine
    Alum in excess.

This solution is exposed to the light for three weeks and 1 per cent. eosin added. The preparations should be stained for 24 hours. The red blood-cells appear a strawberry red, their nuclei, if present, a deep black, the protoplasm of the leucocytes a light lilac and their nuclei a deep lilac. The eosinophilic granules are a brilliant reddish purple, the nuclei of the lymphocytes look dark and their protoplasm is faintly stained.

Ehrlich's tri-acid solution :

Distilled water...............................100
Orange G..135
Acid fuchsin...................................... 65
Distilled water................................100
Absolute alcohol...............................100
Methyl green....................................125
Distilled water................................100
Absolute alcohol...............................100
Glycerine.......................................100

They are gradually mixed together and the solution is allowed to stand for a time. The cover-glasses are kept for five minutes in this solution. The red blood-cells are stained yellow and their nuclei, when present, greenish-blue. The neutrophilic leucocytes show fine violet-colored granules and greenish-blue nuclei. The eosinophilic granules are stained a brilliant red.

Ehrlich's neutral solution :

Saturated aqueous solution of acid fuchsin..........5.
Concentrated aqueous solution of methylene blue....1.
Distilled water..................................5.

Add gradually with continuous shaking to the fuchsin, the solution of methylene blue, then the water, and filter. After standing a few days the solution stains in 5–20 minutes.

Saturated alcoholic solution of dahlia............ 50.
Glacial acetic acid............................... 10.
Distilled water..................................100

Especially recommended for the gamma, basophilic granules.

The author doubts the practical clinical value of this work for the physician, though it may be of use in the laboratory to demonstrate the progressive development of leucocytes or in special researches in certain diseases of the blood. The claim that by this method the different forms of leukæmia can be diagnosticated earlier would hardly compensate for the labor involved in such work when it is considered how rare a disease leukæmia is, occurring only once in sixty thousand cases in Wurzburg, and once in a thousand cases in Vienna. Ehrlich's work, however, has drawn attention to the study of the leucocytes and their increase in number in various morbid conditions. Such investigations seem to point to a field rich in diagnostic and prognostic results.

10. The following is a short summary of the usual condition of the blood found in the various forms of anæmia, necessarily only approximate and in exceptional cases inexact.

CHLOROSIS.—The blood is microscopically evidently paler, and the quantity of hæmoglobin reduced to 50, 40 per cent. and less. The number of red blood-cells is usually normal or slightly diminished, and their shape is generally unchanged. The leucocytes are not increased in number, but at times they may be relatively increased. In severe cases the hæmoglobin is reduced to about 20 per cent (even to 10 per cent.), the number of red blood-cells is markedly diminished (2–3,000,000) and they exhibit marked poikilocytosis.

ANÆMIA.—This is usually a secondary disease, and the changes in the blood depend upon the character and duration of the primary disease (phthisis, carcinoma, syphilis, chronic nephritis, etc.). There is a more or less marked diminution in the number of red blood-cells and a proportionate decrease in hæmoglobin. The number of leucocytes is usually normal, though it may be increased. The shape of the red blood-cells is generally unchanged, but in severe cases there may be marked poikilocytosis, and some of the red blood-cells may be nucleated (Fig. 28, See end of volume.)

PROGRESSIVE PERNICIOUS ANÆMIA.—The red blood-cells are always very much reduced in number, even to less than 1,000,000, and the hæmoglobin is also much diminished, but not to such a degree as the red blood-cells. There is pronounced poikilocytosis with little tendency to the formation of rolls. Many microcytes and numerous megalocytes are seen. Large nucleated red blood-cells are almost always found either in small number or quite numerous. The number of leucocytes is normal though there is a relative increase.

LEUKÆMIA.—In advanced cases the diagnosis is easily made by a superficial microscopical examination of the blood. In the early stage a careful examination is necessary, not only the counting of the red and white blood-cells but also the staining of the dried preparations being then of value. The characteristic of leukæmic blood is the enormous and progressive increase of leucocytes, even to 360,000 from 8–9000, so that the ratio of white to red may be changed from 1 : 550 to 1 : 30, or even 1 : 2 when the number of red cells is greatly reduced. The red blood-cells are paler than normal, variable in size, and usually moderately reduced in number though exceptionally the reduction may be excessive. The diminution in the hæmoglobin generally corresponds to that of the red blood-cells. The leucocytes show striking differences. Small and medium-sized, finely granular leucocytes, and many highly refractive and coarsely granular cells are seen. If the small mononuclear leucocytes (lymphocytes) predominate, the lymph glands are especially involved. If the large cells are the more numerous, the marrow and spleen are the more affected ; the spleen, if in each field there appear 3–5 cells filled with highly refracting granules ; the marrow, if very large mononuclear leucocytes are seen (Fig. 29. See end of volume).

PSEUDO-LEUKÆMIA.—The condition of the blood is similar to that found in secondary anæmia, a variable reduction in the number of red blood-cells, a corresponding diminution in the hæmoglobin, but none of the changes characteristic of leukæmia are present.

Part V.—PATHOLOGICAL FLUIDS.

1. TRANSUDATES are transparent yellow or greenish-yellow alkaline fluids containing few cellular elements (leucocytes, endothelial cells). They do not coagulate spontaneously, or if so only after a time. If they contain blood either through transudation or as a result of the puncture, a gelatinous or membranous coagulation of fibrin results. Old transudates into serous cavities lose this characteristic. Transudates have a low specific gravity and contain albumin (fibrinogen, serum globulin, serum albumin). Both the specific gravity and the quantity of albumin vary, however, with the region of transudation and increase progressively in transudates into the tunica vaginalis, the pleural and peritoneal cavities, the skin, and the cerebral cavities. The other solid constituents are neither important nor characteristic.

2. EXUDATES.—The serous exudates alone need be considered, as the suppurative and hemorrhagic are easily recognized. The exudates are similar in color to the transudates, but contain more cellular elements and are therefore cloudy. They, almost without exception, coagulate either immediately after their evacuation or at the longest after twenty-four hours.

The addition of diluted acetic acid produces a precipitate of a substance similar to globulin, which, in contra-distinction to that formed in the transudates, is dissolved with great difficulty in an excess of the acid, and is insoluble in a solution of sodium chloride. The exudates have a higher specific gravity, contain more albumin than the transudates, and do not vary in these elements. But the differences are not so marked that these two fluids can always be sharply separated from each other. More often there are transitions, *i. e.*, transudates which contain more albumin than the exudate containing the least albumin, and the reverse. Reuss has, however, determined certain limits, the minimum of albumin and of the specific gravity for exudates, and the maximum of the same for transudates.

They are:

	Percentage of albumin.		Specific gravity.	
	Exudate more than	Transudate less than	Exudate higher than	Transudate lower than
Hydrothorax..	4.0	2.5	1018	1015
Ascites	4.0–4.5	1.5–2.0	"	1012
Anasarca......	4.0	1.0–1.5	"	1010
Hydrocephalus.		0.5–1.0	"	1009

The determination of the quantity of albumin or simply of the specific gravity [1] furnishes, when other symptoms fail, an easy method of differentiating a transudate from an exudate. This is the case only when no complications are present.

The most exact method of estimating the albumin is to coagulate it and weigh the coagulum. The approximative methods, given under urinary analysis, can also be used. The specific gravity is determined in the same manner as that of urine. If the fluid is cloudy it should be clarified by standing or by filtration. Clear fluids also should stand for twelve hours, if exact results are desired, as they have a lower specific gravity before the evaporation of the gases which they contain.

3. CONTENTS OF OVARIAN CYSTS.—The contents of ovarian cysts differ much in character, from an aqueous, light-yellow, clear alkaline fluid, to a tough, stringy, mucilaginous body of whitish, dirty-brown, or yellowish-green color. The specific gravity ranges from

---

[1] The specific gravity and the quantity of albumin usually correspond, as albumin is the only solid constituent whose quantity varies. Exceptions occur when large quantities of sugar (diabetes), of urinary elements (uræmia), or of chyle (obstruction in the secretion of milk) pass into the serous cavities.

1002 to 1055, but is usually between 1010 and 1024 ; generally higher than that of exudates and transudates.

The fluid contains albumin (serum globulin and serum albumin) in varying quantities, and always pseudomucin, a body pathognomonic of ovarian fluids, and which gives them their peculiar character—turbid and stringy—when present in large quantity. The aqueous solutions of pseudomucin are mucilaginous, are filtered with difficulty, and have the following chemical relations :

1. Heated to the boiling point : no precipitate.

2. Addition of acetic acid : no precipitate (differentiates it from mucin).

3. The general reactions for albumin :
   Nitric acid.
   Acetic acid + sodium chloride.
   Acetic acid + ferrocyanide of potassium : no precipitate—the solution only becomes more dense.

4. Boiling with Millon's reagent : reddish-brown coloration.

5. Addition of alcohol : a fibrinous precipitate, soluble in water, even after remaining in alcohol for a day.

6. Boiling with diluted mineral acids : formation of a body which can reduce cupric oxide.

If the ovarian fluid contains a large quantity of pseudomucin, it has a thick gelatinous character, and forms, with alcohol, a characteristic fibrinous precipitate. If the quantity of pseudomucin is small, this characteristic is not marked. In such cases, as indeed in all, the following tests should be made if a positive determination is desired :

PSEUDOMUCIN. a. *Heat Test.*—Boil the fluid, which has been faintly acidulated with diluted acetic acid, add carefully a few drops of acetic acid until a flaky precipitate of albumin appears, and proceed exactly as described on page 15. If the filtrate is transparent, no pseudomucin is present ; if the filtrate is whitish, opalescent, pseudomucin may be present. Such a filtrate may be obtained from a solution of pure albumin by the incomplete coagulation of the albumin (compare page 15). Therefore, several tests should be made, and the quantity of acetic acid added to each should be purposely varied. If all the tests give the same result—*i. e.*, a cloudy, opalescent filtrate,—the presence of pseudomucin is probable. The following test is, however, much more delicate :

b. *Reduction Test.*—The filtrate is concentrated on a water bath, and precipitated with alcohol. The flaky precipitate is separated and placed in water. If pseudomucin is present, it is dissolved, making the fluid opalescent. A part of this fluid is submitted to Trommer's test for sugar —*i. e.*, reducing substance. The result will be negative, as reducing substances, if they had been present, would have remained in solution in the alcohol. Add to the rest of the fluid an excess of acetic acid ; if a precipitate (mucin ?) results, it is removed by filtration, and hydrochloric acid to the amount of 5 per cent. is added. The fluid is heated in a test-tube until it becomes a brownish-yellow or brown. It is neutralized with concentrated caustic soda, when cool, and again subjected to Trommer's test. If pseudomucin was originally present, a marked precipitate of cupric suboxide (hamarsten) results. Nylander's test also gives a positive result. If the ovarian fluid is typical, 10 c.c. ($2\frac{1}{2}$ drachms) are sufficient to produce this reduction. If the fluid has the character of water, several hundred c.c. (4–10 ounces) are necessary.

4. CONTENTS OF HYDRONEPHROSIS.—The fluid evacuated in hydronephrosis is usually colorless, transparent, having a specific gravity of 1008 to 1020, and resembles, in its composition, diluted urine. Traces of albumin are often found. Its character is frequently affected by secondary changes ; if mucus or pus is admixed, it is cloudy and contains albumin ; if there is complete anuria, the characteristic urinary elements are absent.

A correct diagnosis by chemical examination is possible only when the characteristic urinary elements (urea and uric acid) are present in large amount. Small amounts have been found in other fluids (urea in echinococcus cysts, uric acid in ascitic fluid in cases of arthritis). The presence of renal epithelium should be carefully looked for in the sediment of the liquid which has been allowed to settle.

UREA.—The fluid is neutralized and evaporated on a water bath until it has, when cool, the consistency of thin syrup. Place a drop on a slide, cover with glass, at the edge of which place a drop of nitric acid. If urea is present, a crystalline precipitate of nitrate of urea is formed, immediately or after some time, at the junction of the fluids. The usual shape is a rhomboidal plate, which at times becomes hexagonal. They generally lie upon one another like slates. This simple method of examination is possible only in fluids which have relatively a large quantity of urea and do not contain albumin and similar substances. In such cases, evaporate the fluid to the consistency of a thick syrup, extract with alcohol, and then evaporate the extract to a like consistency. Crystals of urea (long, thin, four-sided prisms) sometimes appear. Dissolve the sediment, especially the crystallized portion, freed from alcohol by pressing in filtering paper, in water, and test as before for a precipitate of nitrate of urea. If no precipitate results, the fluid does not contain the quantity of urea necessary for the positive diagnosis of hydronephrosis.

URIC ACID.—If the fluid contains albumin, remove it (*vide* page 15). Evaporate the filtrate to a small volume, add, when cool, a few drops of hydrochloric acid, and place in the cold. If uric acid, in not too small a quantity, is present, a crystalline precipitate is formed. This is recognized as uric acid by its form and by the murexide test.

5. ECHINOCOCCUS CYSTS.—The fluid of the echino-

coccus cysts is usually clear, of a neutral or alkaline reaction, of low specific gravity, 1.007–1.015, and contains much sodium chloride, which is crystallized on evaporation. Albumin is usually absent, or only traces are found. If a large quantity of albumin is present, it is due to repeated punctures. Succinic acid is a constant constituent, and its salts are found in small amount. These are detected by a simple method. Evaporate the fluid to the consistency of a syrup, acidulate with hydrochloric acid, and extract with ether. The succinic acid appears as imperfect crystals (large prisms and hexagonal plates) after diluting the ether. Its aqueous solution forms a rusty-colored, flaky, or gelatinous precipitate of succinate of iron with ferric chloride. The hooklets and portions of the echinococcus membrane which are absolutely diagnostic should be sought after.

8

Part VI.—PATHOGENIC MICRO-ORGAN-ISMS.

1. THE BACILLUS TUBERCULOSIS.—The discovery by Koch that a bacillus is the cause of all tubercular processes, has enabled us to determine whether or not a morbid condition is tubercular. This discovery has been of especial value in pulmonary tuberculosis, in the latent forms and in the early stages before the physical signs are well marked. *It can be stated as a clinical law that the presence of this bacillus in the sputum always indicates tuberculosis.*

Their presence, however, in the sputum does not make the prognosis in all cases of pulmonary tuberculosis unfavorable, as such cases may and do recover. Their apparent absence, on the other hand, does not negative the diagnosis of pulmonary tuberculosis, as so few may be present as to escape detection unless repeated and careful examinations have been made.

The tubercle bacilli are short, slender rods 1.5 μ to 3.5 μ (.00006 to .00014 of an inch) in length, approximately about one fourth to one half the diameter of a red blood-cell. They are either quite straight or less often more or less curved, and in pulmonary tuberculosis they are usually found singly or in groups in the small tough greenish-yellow masses which are expectorated. Their detection is made possible by the fact that they retain various aniline dyes longer than the other elements of the sputum when subjected after staining to a decolorizing agent.

PREPARATION OF THE COVER-GLASSES.—Spread the sputum on a dark surface (a dark plate or a glass on a black background), and seek out the small tough greenish-yellow masses. Separate one of these with a needle and smear some of it on an absolutely clean cover-glass, one which has been washed in distilled water, then in alcohol, and carefully dried. Cover this diagonally with a second glass (Fig. 30), carefully press them together between the fingers, making a thin even layer on each glass, then slide them apart. After the cover-glasses have been dried in the air or by gentle heat, *i. e.* held between the fingers at a distance from a flame, pass them, held with forceps, and with besmeared side uppermost, three times through a flame, each transit occupying a little more than a second, to coagulate and thus fix the albumin. The preliminary

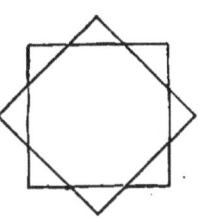

FIG. 30.—ARRANGE-MENT OF COVER-GLASSES.

drying must have been complete or the result will be of less value, as the protoplasm of the bacteria when coagulated at a high temperature loses its normal outline. They are now ready for staining. When stained they are mounted in Canada balsam on a slide and examined under the microscope. An oil-immersion lens and an Abbé condenser should be used, although a lower magnifying power is sometimes sufficient to distinguish them.

STAINING.—Many methods for staining the tubercle bacillus have been recommended and are in use, but that of Ziehl and Neelsen is probably the simplest and gives very satisfactory results.

METHOD OF ZIEHL AND NEELSEN.

STAINING SOLUTION.

Distilled water.	100 C.C.
Alcohol.	10. C.C.
Carbolic acid in crystals.	5 grams.
Fuchsin in substance.	1 gram.

The solution is easily prepared when required by mixing one part of a concentrated alcoholic solution of fuchsin and nine parts of a 5-per-cent. solution of carbolic acid. The cover-glass is floated for five minutes, with besmeared side downwards, in this solution in a porcelain dish, the solution being gently heated to steaming. It is then transferred from the staining solution to a 20-per-cent. solution of nitric acid, or preferably to a 5-per-cent. solution of sulphuric acid, for decolorization. It should be held with forceps and moved gently about in the diluted acid for a few seconds only, until the preparation, which was a deep red, loses its color and becomes yellowish-brown. It is now washed with a diluted (70 per cent.) solution of alcohol renewed several times until the alcohol is no longer discolored, rinsed in water, dried with filtering paper, and mounted in Canada balsam. The bacilli appear as slender red rods, while the other elements are unstained. A contrast stain is easily made by placing the cover-glass after it has been washed with alcohol in a very diluted (1 per cent.) aqueous solution of methylene blue for three minutes. It is then rinsed in water, dried, and mounted. The bacilli remain colored red because when once stained they are affected by another stain only with great difficulty, while the other elements, other bacteria, fungi, mucus, corpuscles, and epithelia are stained blue (Fig. 31).[1]

Gabbet recommends the following solution of methylene blue in sulphuric acid for decolorization and contrast staining after the use of Ziehl's solution :

        Sulphuric acid (25 per cent.)   100 c. c.
        Methylene blue 1–2 grams.

The cover-glasses should remain in this solution 1–2 minutes. This

[1] For illustration see end of volume.

modification, though it simplifies a little the procedure, removes the control of the decolorization which the original method gives.

The part of the staining procedure which many beginners find difficult is the decolorization by the acid, either allowing the cover-glass to remain in the acid solution too long and thus decolorizing also the bacilli, or too short a time and thereby not extracting sufficiently the stain from the other elements. Frequent trials with sputum known to contain bacilli will usually remove this difficulty.

The bacilli of tuberculosis have also been found in the urine, and their presence indicates a tubercular condition of some part of the urinary tract. The attempts at their detection in the urine have been most laborious and usually profitless. Prudden recommends, however, a procedure which renders their detection much more easy. A large quantity of urine, that of one or two days, is allowed to settle for twelve hours in long cylinders of small diameter. The portion deposited is drawn off and still further concentrated by revolving it in the Litten centrifugal machine (Fig. 10) for three minutes. A little of the sediment thus obtained is placed on a cover-glass, which is treated exactly in the manner described for the staining of the bacilli in sputum.

2. MICROCOCCUS GONORRHŒÆ (GONOCOCCUS).—These cocci usually occurring in pairs or in groups of four are, as a rule, flattened on the sides which lie together, being thus "biscuit-shaped" (semmelförmige). Various species of micrococci have this shape, but it is their occurrence with the pus cells which is especially characteristic of gonococci.

A cover-glass is besmeared with a drop of the suspected pus, covered with another glass, separated, dried in the air, and passed three times through the flame as in the preparation of glasses for the detection of the tubercle bacillus.   They are stained quickly with all the basic aniline colors ; gentian violet, methyl violet, fuchsin, and especially well with an aqueous solution of methylene blue. When stained they are rinsed in water, dried, and mounted.   An exceedingly good double stain is obtained by using Czenzynski's solution.

Methylene blue concentrated aqueous solution.......40
One-half per cent. solution of eosin in 70 % alcohol...20
Distilled water................................40

The cover-glasses are stained for five minutes in this solution heated, rinsed in water, dried with filtering paper, and mounted in Canada balsam.   The gonococci and nuclei are stained blue while the cell-body is light red.   (Figure 32.)[1]

3. PLEURISY.—Recent investigations[2] on the bacteriological ætiology of pleurisy have cleared away much of the doubt and uncertainty involving this subject, and have furnished valuable hints as to its prognosis and treatment.   Cases of pleurisy are commonly divided into two classes, according to the character of the exudate.

A. Serous or sero-fibrinous pleurisy.

B. Purulent pleurisy, or empyema.

1. The serous exudates do not, as a rule, contain bacteria.   Many of them, judged by the history of the case, by lesions elsewhere, or by the course of the disease, are probably tubercular.   A very considerable number, however, are not tubercular in origin, and in many of these cases the prognosis is very favorable.

2. The purulent exudates, as a rule, contain bacteria. The pneumococcus, the streptococcus pyogenes, the

---

[1] For illustration see end of volume.

[2] Prudden, "A Study on the Ætiology of Exudative Pleuritis," *New York Medical Journal*, June 24, 1893.

bacillus tuberculosis, and the staphylococcus pyogenes, either alone or in various combinations, are the bacteria commonly found. Of these, the streptococcus pyogenes and the pneumococcus are most often observed, the streptococcus pyogenes being usually found in cases of simple empyema and the pneumococcus most commonly in cases of meta-pneumonic empyema. In putrid purulent exudates, various forms of saprophytic bacteria have been found either alone or associated with the ordinary pyogenic germs.

As the mortality in cases of empyema due to the streptococcus pyogenes is much higher than in those due to the pneumococcus, it is of value for prognosis and for the purpose of determining suitable operative procedure to subject a small portion of the exudate to microscopical examination to ascertain its bacteriological character.

While it is claimed by some investigators that empyema due to the pneumococcus may yield to aspiration, and the empyema associated with the streptococcus pyogenes requires operative procedure, aspiration being insufficient, it at least seems certain that the question of operative procedure is much more urgent in cases associated with the streptococcus than in those in which the pneumococcus or staphylococcus alone is found.

FIG. 33.—STREPTOCOCCI (AFTER DELAFIELD AND PRUDDEN).

3. To determine then the character of an empyema, a test-puncture with a hypodermatic syringe should be made. A little of the pus is dropped on a cover-glass,

which is covered with another glass and treated in the usual manner.

4. The streptococci are spherical cocci, in diameter about one fourth the length of the tubercle bacillus, arranged in chains resembling strings of beads (Fig. 33.) They are readily stained with all the aniline dyes, and especially well with Löffler's alkaline methylene-blue solution.

Concentrated alcoholic solution of methylene blue . . 30
Solution of caustic potash 1 : 10,000 100

The cover-glass is placed in this solution for a minute or two, washed in water, dried, and mounted (Fig. 33).

5. The pneumococci are lance-shaped short rods, often resembling micrococci, and appear generally in pairs or chains of four, enclosed in a capsule (Fig. 34). When stained as Welch recommends, the capsules are distinctly shown. Glacial acetic acid is dropped upon the cover-glass and after a few seconds is allowed to run off, not washed off with water ; anilin - gentian - violet solution [1] is now poured upon it, successive portions being applied for

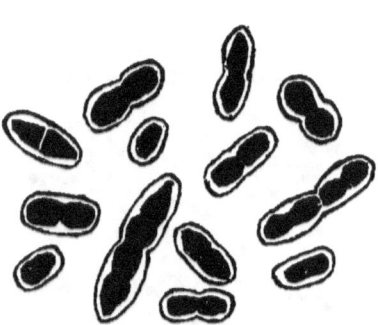

FIG. 34.—PNEUMOCOCCI FROM A CASE OF EMPYEMA.

---

[1] 5 c.c. aniline oil are added to 100 c.c. of distilled water, shaken for some time and then filtered through moistened filtering paper. The filtrate should be perfectly clear, should contain no drops of oil, and should not become opaque when shaken. Otherwise it must be refiltered. To 100 c.c. of the filtrate add 10 c.c. of absolute alcohol and 11 c.c. of the concentrated alcoholic solution of gentian-violet.

4-5 minutes until the acetic acid is displaced. It is then rinsed in a 2-per-cent. solution of salt (NaCl), mounted and examined in this solution of salt (Fig. 34).

4. DIPHTHERIA.—THE USE OF BACTERIAL CULTURES FOR THE DIFFERENTIAL DIAGNOSIS BETWEEN TRUE DIPHTHERIA AND OTHER PSEUDO-MEMBRANOUS INFLAMMATIONS.

It may be considered as fully proven that true diphtheria depends upon the bacilli first described by Klebs and Löffler and that those pseudo-membranes and exudates in which the diphtheria bacilli are absent and only various forms of cocci present are not the lesions of true diphtheria, but of an entirely different disease.

1. THE DIPHTHERIA BACILLI.—They are straight or slightly curved rods nearly as long and often twice as broad as the tubercle bacilli. Sometimes they are of the same width throughout their whole length, while at other times they are pointed or clubbed at their ends (Fig. 35). Though the different bacilli differ greatly in cultures taken from different cases, yet they all have certain class characteristics : when examined on a cover-glass they are found singly or in pairs and have no spores ; injected into guinea-pigs they cause death within a few days, and when inoculated upon

FIG. 35.—PURE CULTURE DIPHTHERIA BACILLI FROM SERUM CULTURE FROM THROAT. X 2,000 DIAM.

the mucous membrane of the trachea produce a true pseudo-membrane. The bacilli grow best at the body temperature, but thrive well between 90° and 100° F. The best medium for their growth is solidified blood scrum, especially that prepared after Löffler's formula (3

parts blood serum, one part nutrient bouillon, to which
1-per-cent glucose has been added). The bacilli usually
grow well on alkaline nutrient agar, especially with the
addition of 6 per cent. of glycerine. The best staining
fluid is Löffler's methyl-blue solution :

Saturated alcoholic solution of methyl blue ....30 parts
Aqueous solution potassium hydrate 1:10,000...70   "

Stained with this fluid the bacilli usually present a
very characteristic appearance. Different portions of
the bodies of the bacilli stain unequally, and the ends
are usually more darkly stained than the bodies. In some
cases the whole bacillus is equally stained.

2. PSEUDO-DIPHTHERIA BACILLI.—This name has
been given to two different kinds of bacteria, neither of
which has any connection with the disease pseudo-diphtheria. The first variety is a bacillus which is in every
way similar to the diphtheria bacillus, except that when
injected subcutaneously in guinea-pigs it does not cause
death. This bacillus is now believed to be the true
diphtheria bacillus which has lost its virulence. The
second variety is a bacillus which is smaller than the
Löffler bacillus, stains more evenly with the methyl blue,
and belongs apparently to a different kind of bacteria.

3. THE STREPTOCOCCI AND OTHER COCCI FOUND IN
THE EXUDATES AND PSEUDO-MEMBRANES.—These appear to be the same as those usually present in healthy
throats. They are minute spheres averaging about one
seventh the diameter of a red blood-cell. When examined on a cover-glass the cocci are found to be
arranged in longer or shorter chains, as diplococci, and
as staphylococci. All forms grow readily on the usual

media and thrive best at a body temperature. They stain readily by the usual dyes.

4. THE PRACTICAL VALUE OF CULTURES.—Recent investigations have brought out the great importance of determining the presence or absence of the diphtheria bacillus in the exudate of an inflamed throat, for it has been found that a considerable proportion of inflammations of the throat commonly considered as diphtheria are not such, while many believed during the first days or even throughout the whole disease to be only benign in character are found to be true diphtheria.

The differential diagnosis, often so difficult clinically, is readily made with cultures within twelve hours. The cultures should be made as early in the disease as possible, not only for the importance of quickly recognizing those cases which are true diphtheria so that we may prevent the spreading of the disease, but also because in the milder cases of true diphtheria the bacilli themselves may disappear from the throat after four or five days. Cultures are also of value in convalescence, to determine when the patient ceases to be a danger to others.

5. THE METHODS USED TO DETERMINE THE PRESENCE OF THE BACILLI IN THE THROAT.—The attempt has been made to directly smear some of the exudate from the throat on a slide, dry it, stain with methyl blue, and examine. In a certain number of cases, the bacilli are so abundant and so typical that a quick diagnosis can thus be obtained, but there are many others in which it is impossible to make a diagnosis in this way. The slower but sure method by cultures has therefore been adopted by all investigators, and is employed either alone or in addition to the direct microscopical examination of the exudate.

To obtain a culture, the best materials are a tube containing sterile, slanted, solidified blood-serum, and a steel rod or stick armed with a sterile cotton swab, which is kept in a second tube. The patient should be placed in the best light possible and properly held. In cases where it is easy to get a good view of the throat, rub the cotton swab gently but freely against any visible exudate. In other cases, including those in which the exudate is confined to the larynx, open the mouth, pass the swab back till it reaches the pharynx, and then rub it freely against the muçous membrane of the pharynx or tonsils. Without laying the swab down, withdraw the cotton plug from the culture tube, insert the swab and rub that portion of it which has touched the exudate gently back and forth along the surface of the blood-serum. Then replace the swab in its own tube, and plug both tubes with the cotton. The inoculated tube is now to be kept for ten to twelve hours at a temperature between 90° and 100° F. It is then ready for examination. On inspection, the blood-serum surface will be seen to be dotted with very numerous, just visible, translucent colonies. At this time no diagnosis can be made from simple inspection. A clean cover-glass with a tiny drop of water having been prepared, a platinum wire is inserted in the blood-serum tube and a sweep made of a large number of colonies. The bacteria adherent to the wire are washed off in the drop on the cover-glass and smeared over its surface. After drying, it is carried quickly through the Bunsen flame three times, then covered with a few drops of Löffler's solution of alkaline methyl blue, and left for five minutes. The cover-glass is then rinsed off in clean water, and either examined in water on the slide or dried and mounted in balsam.

In the great majority of cases, one of two pictures will be seen with the oil-immersion lens : either an enormous number of one of the characteristic forms of the diphtheria bacilli, with or without a moderate number of diplo- or streptococci (Fig. 35), or a pure culture of cocci mostly in pairs and chains. In a few there will be an approximately even mixture of Löffler bacilli and cocci (Fig. 36), and in some with the cocci there will be a moderate number of bacilli in chains or scattered, some resembling a little, and others not at all, the Löffler bacilli (Fig. 37).

 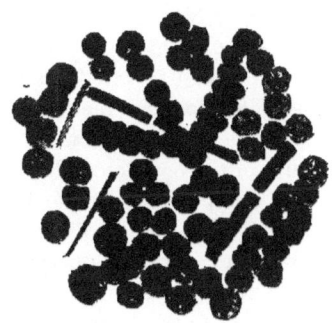

FIG. 36.—MIXED CULTURE OF COCCI AND DIPHTHERIA BACILLI.   FIG. 37.—CULTURE OF VARIOUS FORMS OF COCCI, AND A FEW NON-PATHOGENIC BACILLI.

The question will be asked, how much knowledge of bacteriology is it necessary for a physician to have in order to make the cultures and the microscopical examinations? Any one who is accustomed to examine sputa for the tubercle bacillus, and is able to clearly tell a bacillus from a coccus, can easily make a positive diagnosis in nine tenths of the cases, if he carefully follows the instructions here given, and is supplied with a good oil-immersion lens. It will help him greatly in his first case if he has previously studied cover-glass preparations of the stained diphtheria bacilli.

The diagnosis of true diphtheria is certain in those cases in which a great number of bacilli resembling those of diphtheria are present in the cultures (Fig. 36), while in those in which no bacilli but only cocci are found, the diagnosis of false diphtheria is equally sure, if the culture was made during the first days of the disease and no antiseptic had just previously been applied. Those in which, among numerous kinds of cocci, there are a few bacilli which look somewhat like the diphtheria bacilli and yet are not characteristic, are very difficult to diagnosticate (Fig. 37). Those who have had little experience had better simply consider these from the bacterial standpoint as suspicious cases, and give no positive opinion.

The absence of diphtheria bacilli in cultures made from throats in which the disease was confined to the larynx does not absolutely exclude the diagnosis of true diphtheria.

6. A READY METHOD FOR PREPARING THE MATERIALS AND APPARATUS NEEDED FOR DIPHTHERIA CULTURES.—Blood-serum is obtained by catching the blood directly from a slaughtered sheep or steer into large covered, clean glass jars or pails. The blood is allowed to clot and then kept on ice for twenty-four hours. The serum is then syphoned off by a rubber tube and mixed with one third its bulk of the bouillon. The bouillon is made by soaking one pound of raw chopped beef in one litre of water for twelve hours in a cool place. This is then strained through cheese-cloth and to it is added one-per-cent. peptone, one-per-cent. glucose, and one-half-per-cent. salt. The whole is boiled for one half hour, filtered, and is then ready to be added to the serum. The necessary number of short wide test-tubes, having been previously plugged with cotton, and if possible sterilized by dry heat, are now filled to the height of one inch with the serum mixture and put in a slanting position on a serum coagulator, or when this is not at hand in the inner vessel of a double boiler. This is now kept just below the boiling temperature for an hour. The tubes are then allowed to cool, and then heated for the same length of time the following day. The serum is thus firm and sterile. The tubes are stored in a tin box, and remain for months ready for use. The swabs are most neatly made from 6-inch pieces of steel wire. One end is roughened and wound tightly with a very little absorbent cotton. This placed in a tube is then sterilized. A perfectly satisfactory incubator can be made from a double boiler. The upper vessel is weighted with lead or sand sufficient to hold it down when the lower vessel is full of water. The tin cover is replaced by a board which has been perforated at its centre for the insertion of a thermometer. The whole can be covered with asbestos. A Bunsen burner, the outer tube of which has been removed, makes a satisfactory burner. Even without a regulator, the gas can be so adjusted that the temperature of the incubator will not vary too greatly from 98° F. for use.

5. AMŒBA COLI.—Osler describes the amœba as a unicellular protoplasmic motile organism from 10 to 20 μ diameter (2–3 times the size of a red blood-cell), consisting of a clear outer zone, ectosarc, and a granular inner zone, endosarc containing a nucleus and one or more vacuoles (Fig. 38).

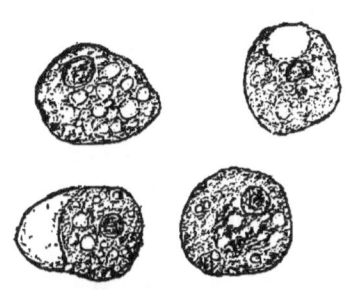

They are present constantly in the stools, in the intestines, and in the complicating liver abscesses in the endemic dysentery of Egypt, and have also been found in this country in a number of cases of

FIG. 38.—AMŒBA COLI (AFTER DELAFIELD AND PRUDDEN).

dysentery reported by Osler, Councilman, Lafleur, Dock, Musser, and others. The amœbæ are more numerous in the small gelatinous masses often contained in the fæces, but their numbers vary in different cases and even in the same case at different times, although they are usually proportional to the severity of the disease. Their appearance differs according to their state ; activity or inactivity. When inactive they are round, slightly oblong, more refractive than other cells found in the fæces, and contain vacuoles of varying size. The vacuoles are clear and their contents paler than the surrounding substance. When active they have a characteristic appearance due to a double movement : progressive, and one limited to the protrusion and retraction of pseudopodia.

In seeking the amœba, Councilman advises that attention should be paid to the following points.

1. The stools are to be passed into a warm bed-pan and kept at a temperature of 30° to 35° C. (86°–93° F.) until an examination is made.

2. The examination should be made as soon as possible, before the stools become acid.

3. The small gelatinous masses, which contain amœbæ in greatest abundance, should be carefully examined.

A magnifying power of 400 is most suitable, though they may be found with a magnifying power of 100 diameters. Some form of warm stage is essential if the observation is to be continued.

This form of dysentery is characterized by a variable onset, irregular course, frequent intermissions and exacerbations, and by a tendency to chronicity. The main characteristic of the stools is their fluidity. They may or may not at first contain blood, but later both blood and mucus are almost always present. From six to twelve yellowish-gray stools are passed daily for weeks. Abscess of the liver is a frequent and serious complication. The stools in all cases of prolonged diarrhœa should be carefully examined for amœbæ.

6. PLASMODIUM MALARIÆ.—The fact that malaria is due to the presence of a parasite in the blood was first definitely determined by Laveran. His discovery has been confirmed by Italian observers and by numerous workers in the United States. These micro-organisms are protozoa, belong to the division known as hæmatozoa, and are found in the red blood-cells.

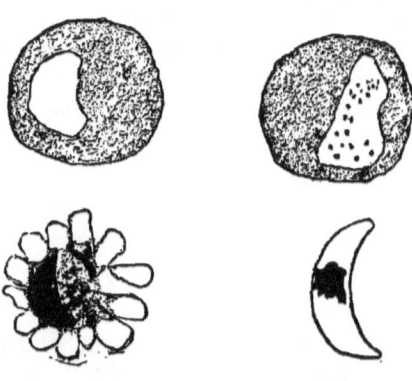

FIG. 39.—PLASMODIUM MALARIÆ.

The following are the forms representing stages in their life history as described by American observers. The parasite, however, assumes a variety of forms in cases in the same locality and shows marked variations in different countries.

1. An unpigmented hyaline body within the red blood-cells. (Fig. 39.)

2. A pigmented amœboid body within the red blood-cells. (Fig. 39.)

3. A segmenting body more or less perfect which breaks up into a varying number of small spheroids (spores). (Fig. 39.)

4. Crescents containing pigment. (Fig. 39.)

5. Flagellate organisms which develop from the inter-cellular pigmented forms or from ovoid bodies which are altered crescents.

6. Free flagella.

Golgi has described two varieties of this parasite : one, in which the pigment granules are finer and the spheroids more numerous, 15–20, he associates with the tertian type of malaria ; and the other, in which the pigment granules are coarser and the spheroids less numerous, 6–12, with the quartan type. The other types of malaria, he claims, are simply modifications or combinations of these two.

The blood for examination should be obtained at the height of the chill, in the manner described under blood examinations (page 101). It is readily stained by gently heating for 10 to 15 minutes in Czenzynski's solution (page 103). The plasmodia are stained blue, the red blood-cells and the bodies of the leucocytes a light red, their nuclei a deep blue, and the eosinophilic granules of the leucocytes a deed red. As the plasmodia rapidly disappear after the administration of quinine, the preparations of blood should be obtained before quinine is administered.

APPENDIX I.

REAGENTS NECESSARY.

(A) in the examination of the urine :

1 Concentrated yellow nitric acid.
2   "   acetic acid.
3   "   hydrochloric acid.
4   "   sulphuric acid.
5 Caustic soda (liq. sodæ), a solution containing 15 per cent. of sodium hydrate.
6 Saturated solution of salt (Na Cl).
7 Calx chlorata, a half-saturated solution ; made by diluting a saturated solution of chlorinated lime with an equal volume of water. This solution should be renewed from time to time.
8 Chloride of iron (liq. ferri sesquichloridi). It should have an acid reaction, but must be free from acid and should always give a precipitate (iron hydroxide) upon the addition of a drop of aqua ammonia.
9 Ferrocyanide of potassium, 10-per-cent. solution.
10 Sulphate of copper, 10-per-cent. solution.
11 Fehling's solutions.
12 Aqua ammoniæ, 10 per cent. NH_3.
13 Lugol's solution, an aqueous solution of iodine in iodide of potassium.
14 Millon's reagent. Dissolve one part of mercury in an equal part of nitric acid and dilute with twice its bulk of water, then separate, after some hours, by filtration, the reagent from the precipitate.
15 Double solution of iodide of potassium and biniodide of mercury. The biniodide of mercury is dissolved in a warm solution of iodide of potassium to saturation and diluted with several volumes of water.

16 Nitrate of silver, 5-per-cent. solution.   Keep in dark bottle.
17 Alcohol, 90 per cent.
18 Chloroform.
19 Ether.
   Other solutions as needed.

(B) In the examination of the stomach contents :
1 Iodide of potassium in keratin-coated pills.
2 Salol.
3 Methyl-aniline.
4 Congo paper.
5 Tropæolin OO.
6 Vanilla.
7 Phloroglucin.
8 Resorcin.
9 Carbolic acid (liquid).
10 Carmine fibrin.
11 Egg albumin.

(C) In the examination for micro-organisms :
1 Conc. alcohol sol. of fuchsine.
2 "   "   " " methylene blue.
3 " aqueous "   "   "   "
4 One-half-per-cent. sol. of eosin in 70 per cent. alcohol.
5 Solution of caustic potash (1:10,000).
6 Czenzynski's solution.
7 Glacial acetic acid.

(D) In the examination of blood :
1 Solution of sodium chloride 3 %.
2   "   " acetic acid .3-.5 %.
   Ehrlich's solutions.

Apparatus necessary :
   Test-tubes, watch glasses, porcelain dishes, conical glasses, glass funnels, glass rods, platinum foil, retort stand, water bath, iron tripod, litmus paper, urinometer, stomach tube, slides, glasses, apparatus for examination of blood, microscope with suitable objectives.

APPENDIX II.

Metric Weights and Measures employed in this book with their equivalents in grains, or minims :

		Gram.		Grains.
Milligram	=	.001	=	.01543
Centigram	=	.01	=	.1543
Decigram	=	.1	=	1.5432
Gram	=	1.	=	15.43235

		Metre.		Inches.
Micromillimetre (μ)	=	.000001	=	.00004
Millimetre	=	.001	=	.03937
Centimetre	=	.01	=	.3937
Decimetre	=	.1	=	3.937
Metre	=	1.	=	39.37

		Cubic inches.		Minims.
Cubic millimetre	=	.00006	=	.01622
Cubic centimetre (c. c.)	=	.0610165	=	16.22

				Quart.
Litre (1000 c. c.)	=	61.	=	.946

Fahrenheit and Centigrade thermometric scales compared and formulæ for converting the registration of one into that of the other :

Fahr.		Cent.
212 °	=	100 °
160 °	=	71.1 °
120 °	=	48.9 °
100 °	=	37.8 °
80 °	=	26.7 °
60 °	=	15.6 °
32 °	=	0. °
0 °	=	17.8 °

To convert Fahrenheit scale to Centigrade :

$$C = \frac{5 \, (F - 32)}{9}$$

To convert Centigrade scale to Fahrenheit :

$$F = \frac{9 \, C}{5} + 32$$

FIG. 5.—PHENYL-GLUCOSAZON (JAKSCH).

A few needles may be found in any specimen of urine, with heaps of yellow amorphous granules and brownish-red scales.

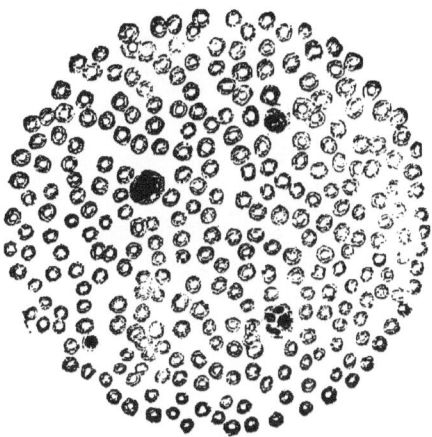

FIG. 27.—STAINED PREPARATION OF NORMAL BLOOD.

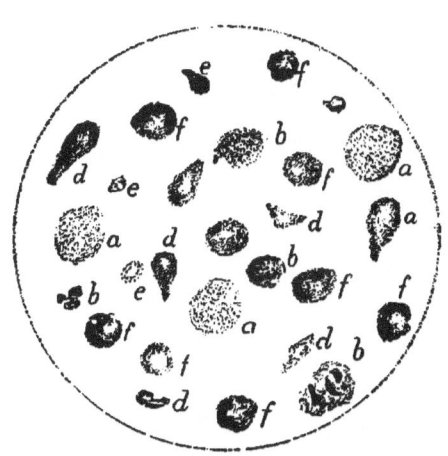

FIG. 28.—ANÆMIC BLOOD STAINED BY EHRLICH'S METHOD
(AFTER V. LIMBECK).

a, megalocytes ; b, leucocytes (different kinds) ; d, poikilocytes ;
e, mycrocytes ; f, normal red blood cells.

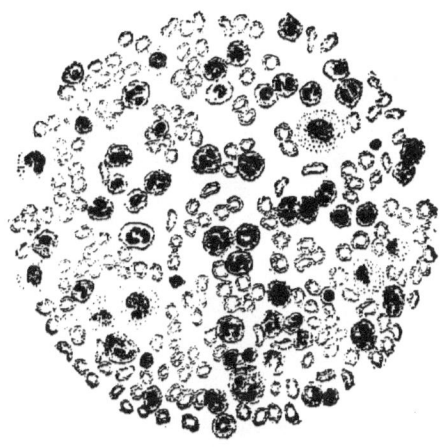

FIG. 29 · LEUKÆMIC BLOOD STAINED WITH EOSIN AND
HÆMOTOXYLON.

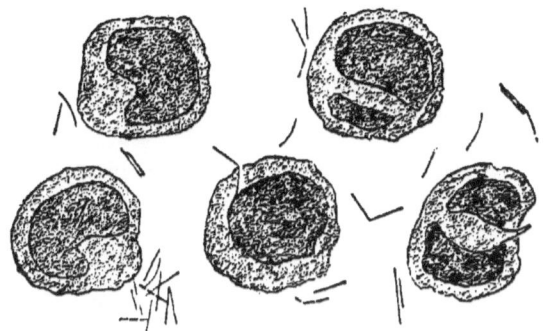

FIG. 31.—TUBERCLE BACILLI FROM SPUTUM.

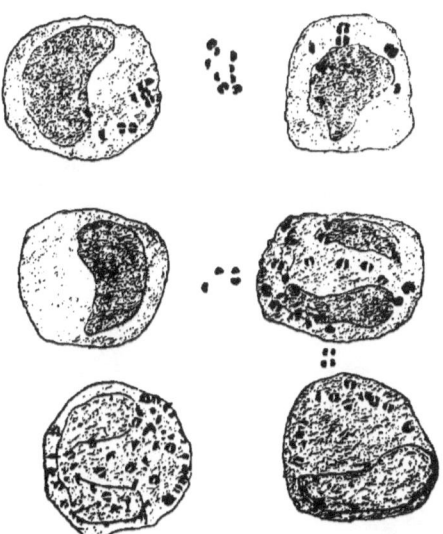

FIG. 32.—MICROCOCCI GONORRHŒÆ
(GONOCOCCI).

INDEX.